BORROW MY HEART

ALSO BY KASIE WEST

BORROW MY HEART

KASIE WEST

DELACORTE PRESS

Text copyright © 2023 by Kasie West
Jacket art copyright © 2023 by Charley Clements

All rights reserved. Published in the United States by Delacorte Press, an imprint of Random House Children's Books, a division of Penguin Random House LLC, New York.

Delacorte Press is a registered trademark and the colophon is a trademark of Penguin Random House LLC.

GetUnderlined.com

Educators and librarians, for a variety of teaching tools, visit us at RHTeachersLibrarians.com

Library of Congress Cataloging-in-Publication Data is available upon request.
ISBN 978-0-593-64325-9 (tr. pbk.) — ISBN 978-0-593-64326-6 (ebook)

The text of this book is set in 11.2-point Adobe Garamond Pro.
Interior design by Cathy Bobak

Printed in the United States of America
1st Printing
First Edition

No dogs die in this book! But sometimes, in real life, they do. To our sweet rescue, Harley. Thanks for making our lives better and for always being the Goodest Boy.

CHAPTER 1

· · · · · · · · · · · · · · · ·

Rule: *Never date a guy you just met. He could just
as likely be a sociopath as a nice guy.*

"Hey," I said, sliding my beach tote off my shoulder and onto the
checkered tile floor of the coffee shop. "I thought you were off
at four."

Kamala, my best friend, sighed from behind the register. "Lewis
called in sick, so Meg asked if I would stay."

"Your mean boss asked you to stay and you said, 'Screw Wren,
of course I can stay.'"

"Shh!" She looked over her shoulder toward the back hall, then
flicked something off the counter at me. "I know, I'm messing up
your perfectly planned afternoon."

Her ammunition hit my shoulder, then landed on the ground.
"What was that?" I squinted at the floor. "A piece of muffin?"

"Chocolate chip." The coffee shop where Kamala worked also
sold baked goods, displayed behind lit glass.

I picked up the chocolate chip and tossed it in the trash. "When
are you off?"

"Six."

"Six? You don't want to go to the beach anymore?" There went my afternoon plans.

She rolled her eyes. "It's not like you were going to get in the water anyway, Ocean Hater."

"I put my feet in! Do you know how many predators live in the ocean?"

"Not *your* predators, Wren."

"You're the one who showed me that video of the whale swallowing a kayaker."

"She was just in the way of real food. It spit her out."

"It spit her out? *That's* your swim-in-the-ocean pitch? I'm good, thanks." I tugged out my ponytail holder and redid my messy bun in the reflection of a framed photo of a surfboard hanging on the wall. "What about that great white that ate that man six months ago right here on our beach? It's still out there with the taste of human blood in its mouth."

"You're more likely to get struck by lightning than attacked by a shark."

"And you don't see me walking around with a metal rod, do you?"

Kamala shook her head. "The beach will still exist in a couple hours, you know. We can go watch the sunset, bury our feet in the sand. It will be so romantic," she teased. "It's been a while since you've had that in your life."

"It *has* been a while since I've had sand all over my feet."

She ignored my sarcasm. "How long ago was Phillip, anyway?

Last year? Not that he ever made it to boyfriend status. It's your stupid list of rules. Nobody will ever measure up."

"Then I guess I'll die alone." I smirked and walked to my favorite table, tucked around the corner from the register, out of the way. This little nook of the café had tall wood bookshelves filled with knickknacks, potted plants, and a dozen or so self-help books (most about cultivating a positive attitude through yoga or bird-watching or self-hypnosis). If I was hanging out here for a couple of hours, I could read while Kamala helped customers. Reading was one of the things I had planned for the beach anyway. It wasn't that I couldn't go with the flow of a new schedule . . . okay, it sort of was. I liked my life planned. It ran better that way.

The bell on the door dinged and two guys, who I could just make out through the broad-leafed plant on the counter, walked in. I slunk into a chair. One of the guys was holding his phone as if he was taking a selfie. But then he started talking.

"Today is the moment of truth, Asher. Here, in this cheesy beach-themed coffee shop"—he pointed his phone at a big seashell plastered to the wall—"I will be proven right and you will be sad you ever made an official bet with me."

The guy without the phone—Asher, apparently—gave a good-natured smile as the phone was pointed at him, and approached the counter.

I had not been planning on staying, so I was wearing leggings and a sweatshirt over my swimsuit. I slouched deeper into the chair and pretended to look through my bag as the two guys ordered coffee.

"You didn't have to come," Asher said. He was a lanky white guy wearing glasses and a beanie. He produced a twenty-dollar bill out of his pocket and handed it to Kamala.

"But then how would I record your humiliation for future generations?" Phone Guy was taller and wore a *Star Wars* T-shirt and Docs. And he was *still* recording. "Besides, you think this little girl is going to save you from internet predators?" He nodded toward Kamala.

"Little *woman*," she corrected in her sassy yet disarming way. "And I won't." She handed him the receipt with a pile of change sitting on top. "We don't even have a panic button here."

Phone Guy finally lowered his phone. "You shouldn't volunteer that information to strangers."

"I'm trusting," Kamala said. She really was. But she was also a good judge of character. I was her best friend, after all.

"Oh, kind of like you, Asher," Phone Guy said. "You share everything with everyone."

Asher pushed his glasses up his nose and smiled like it was a compliment. He slid the change off the receipt and into the tip jar.

"Do you have a question for my friend?" Phone Guy said to Kamala. "He will tell you anything. Want to know his shoe size?"

He pointed to Asher, who said, "Twelve."

"Height?"

"Six one," Asher said.

Phone Guy lowered his brow like he didn't quite believe him, but continued with, "Favorite childhood trauma?"

Asher opened his mouth like he was actually going to answer

when his friend saved him with, "Never mind. Everyone knows you had a perfect childhood anyway."

Kamala held up a Sharpie and a coffee cup. "Um . . . how about just a name."

"Dale," Phone Guy said.

"Oh, I see how it is," Asher said. "I pay, you take the credit."

Dale, not humoring his joke with a response, pointed at the small wooden box on the counter. "What's that?"

"It's a suggestion box," Kamala said. She hated that suggestion box; most of the time it was full of pickup lines or rude comments.

"Old-school feedback," Asher said with a nod. "Nice." He ripped a piece of paper off the pad beside the box, wrote something down, then dropped the paper in the slot on top. Then he looked around the café. I ducked my head. His eyes didn't even pause on me. *Saved by the overgrown counter plant.* He pointed toward the only booth, next to the window where someone had painted a summery scene—the ocean, a colorful umbrella, flip-flops, a striped towel.

How long has that been there? It was barely the first week of summer. Had Kamala painted it?

The guys walked to the booth and sat. The hissing of the cappuccino machine muffled the conversation across the room. I dug my car keys out of my bag, thinking maybe I'd leave after all.

"So?" Kamala asked, shifting to the side counter and leaning over it so she could talk quietly. "Sunset on the beach with your bestie? I mean, I meet all your very specific criteria for love, right?" She placed a hand under her chin like she was putting her face on display. Kamala was gorgeous. She was Indian, with thick, straight black hair, dark intense eyes, a regal nose, and full lips. "Now that I think about it, I probably don't. I haven't read your rules lately."

And she wouldn't read them. Ever again. She'd already made fun of them enough, and that was before I added my post-Phillip criteria: *must know a guy for six months before I consider dating him, must know for a fact that he gets along with at least one family member, and he must have one or more friends he's known and kept since elementary school.* I didn't think those were unfair additions. They were common sense, really—the reasons Phillip definitely wasn't boyfriend material. "Of course you meet the criteria. You're my one and only."

Kamala curled her lip. "That's really . . ."

"Sweet?" I asked with a smirk.

"Pathetic." The machine stopped hissing and Kamala tightened a lid on the cup. "Dale!" she called out like there were more than just two other people in the café.

Dale stood and walked over. He gave Kamala a lazy smile as he picked up the two drinks.

"Thanks," he said, and carried them back to the table.

Now that it was quiet again, I could hear them.

"What time did she say she'd be here?" Dale asked. "Because I am so ready to win this bet and watch you make a fool of yourself at my birthday party."

"You will not win this bet. She's coming." Asher looked at his phone. "Any minute now."

"You said four, right? It's after four. I still haven't decided what would embarrass you more. Streaking butt naked around the yard three times with the whole school watching or performing that dance you learned in the third grade."

Asher took off his beanie, revealing a beautiful wavy mess of auburn hair, and put it on the table. If I had that hair, I would never cover it with a hat. My hair was stick straight and plain brown. "Neither of those would embarrass me," he said.

Even I could tell he was bluffing. His cheeks had gone a little red and his shoulders slumped.

Dale just laughed and pointed his phone at him again like he was recording his embarrassment. *Is he?*

Asher held up his hand, blocking the camera. "You don't need to think of anything, she's coming."

"And how are we going to know it's her when she walks in? You've never met this girl and have zero pics of her."

"I'll know," Asher said.

Dale scoffed. "By the magic of your underdeveloped intuition?"

"Thanks for the support," Asher said.

"But, seriously," Dale responded. "Tell me you've spoken to her. Like actually heard her voice."

Asher gave an eye roll with his whole head. "Stop recording me."

"Kamala," I whispered. She looked over from where she was straightening napkins but obviously eavesdropping as well. It wasn't like they were talking quietly. "What rhymes with rat-dished?"

"Don't be mean, Wren."

I didn't think it was mean. The guy's friend seemed like the mean one, thinking up ways to humiliate him for fun.

Dale continued, "I will stop recording when you do any sort of video call with this girl."

"I'll do better," Asher said. "I'll talk to her in person when she walks through that door." He stared at the door as though him saying it would make her magically appear.

Dale burst out laughing. I shivered, the laugh triggering me. My mom used to do that: laugh when I was uncomfortable, laugh when I was hurt, laugh when I asked a question she didn't want to answer.

"Asher, dude, it's over. You can admit it," Dale said through his laughter. "I've played along this far, but you don't really think she's coming, do you? I know Elinor did a number on you, but are you really this stupid?"

I shot to my feet, almost involuntarily. My chest was burning. "Can I use the break room?" I asked Kamala under my breath.

"Why?" she asked warily.

"Can I?"

"Yes."

I picked up my tote, rounded the counter, and went down the hall as casually as possible. Meg exited the kitchen just as I reached the break room. Her eyes went from my messy bun to my flip-flops. She had a sour look on her face that I knew was more stress than actual meanness. I thought about suggesting one of the books on her shelf—yoga or self-hypnosis—but decided not to press my luck.

"Can I help you?" she asked.

"I spilled something on my shirt, I wanted to change."

She gave a single nod. "Don't linger."

"No, yes, I mean, thank you, I won't." I pointed to the door and rushed around her.

I stepped into the break room and dug the change of clothes I had brought for after the beach out of my bag—a pair of jean shorts and a striped crop top. Kamala appeared just as I stripped off my sweatshirt.

"What are you doing?" She was obviously shocked. I was a little too. I wasn't typically impulsive. I tried very hard not to be, in fact.

"I'm helping." I peeled off my leggings and pulled on my shorts.

"What? Helping who?"

"That guy out there has been talking to a girl he's never met. *I'm* a girl he's never met."

Kamala's eyebrows pulled together as she took in my meaning. "He doesn't need you to save him from his own friend."

"It's not about him. I'm saving *us* from having to sit through more of this secondhand embarrassment." Seriously, the humiliation his friend was threatening to put him through had sent tension through my whole body.

"What if this girl, whoever she is, isn't a catfish?"

I turned the crop top so that the tag was in the back and put my arms in the sleeves. "She is. And if I don't do this, she'll come up with some excuse for today and keep dragging him along for weeks and weeks."

"What if she's just late and shows up while you're out there pretending to be her?"

"That will be awkward." I pulled the shirt over my head, tugging it down over my swimsuit top. "Did he say her name? What's my name supposed to be?"

"I heard no name."

I used the mirror on the wall to apply a coat of mascara. I took the ponytail holder out of my hair, flipped my head upside down, ran my fingers through my long brown locks, then flipped back up.

The bell on the door let out a ding. "Let's hope that's her," Kamala said. "Or they got impatient and left."

I shrugged. Those would also be perfectly fine endings to this scenario. I really didn't care about him. I didn't know him. I cared about this stupid feeling that had taken over my body, reminding me that even though my mother was four hundred miles away, she still seemed to have a hold on my emotions. *I* was in charge of my feelings. Not the memory of things she had done and definitely not her.

"This is a really terrible idea," Kamala said.

"Can you think of a better one?" I asked.

"Yes! Just sit there and let it play out on its own."

"That wasn't working at all," I said. "I've already decided." And once I made a decision, I always followed through with it.

Kamala knew this as well and gave a long-suffering sigh, resigned. "You're such a control freak."

"That's why you love me." I reached into her pocket, where I knew she kept a tube of sparkly pink lip gloss. I applied a coat to my lips, then blew her a kiss as I headed for the back door. "You better get out there for the show."

CHAPTER 2

· · · · · · · · · · · · · · · ·

Rule: *Never date a guy who thinks everything is a sign. Finding a note that says It's Tuesday! is only a miracle on a Tuesday.*

I could still back out. All I had to do was walk across the room, order a coffee, and ignore the guys, who had gone completely silent in the booth to my right. I had exited the café out the back, avoided a muddy puddle in the west alley, and come in through the front, where I paused, one hand behind me still gripping the door. The little bell around the handle had gone silent, too, after its initial cheery jingle. Kamala gave me an eyebrow raise from where she was helping a middle-aged man at the counter as if she thought I was chickening out. I wasn't. I'd had the whole walk to turn around. But the walk had only pumped more blood through my veins, and I was more determined now than I'd been ten minutes ago.

I unleashed my full smile, pretended to search the room, before letting my gaze find the table. Would his catfish know which one of these two guys was Asher? My brain quickly decided that she would. He had probably been an open book, like Dale had

11

said he was, sharing selfies and his social media. I locked eyes with him and let my smile soften as if recognition was taking over my expression.

His eyes darted to Kamala, or maybe the empty nook where I'd been sitting before, or maybe to nothing in particular. Then his eyes shot to Dale before he stood in one quick, jerky motion. "Gemma?" he all but whispered.

Gemma? Her name was Gemma? And he thought she was real without actual proof? I was allowed to be skeptical of odd names, I had one, after all.

I took one step in his direction and he somehow shimmied out of the corner seat of the booth and was in front of me in record time. "Hi," I said.

Instead of answering he wrapped me in a hug. "I told you I'd hug you when I saw you," he said against my temple.

He smelled really good, like soap and cinnamon. And he felt even better, his arms putting the perfect amount of pressure against my back, his shoulder the perfect height for my cheek. I hadn't expected him to be such a good hugger. He looked too lanky to feel so significant against me. For the first time since I'd been forced into action, the tightness in my chest loosened. I let out an involuntary sigh, then lowered my brow. *What kind of reaction was that?* My shoulders went tense and he released me.

His confidence was back as he faced Dale.

"This is Gemma." He put his hand on my lower back and it felt warm and sure. "Gemma, this is Dale."

"Nice to meet you," I said.

12

Dale's mouth was open in shock, his phone pointing at the table, recording the Formica top. So much for his perfect video. I considered that my first victory.

"Scoot," Asher said to Dale.

Dale slid down the bench. "You're late," he said, his shocked look turning into a skeptical one.

"Dale, don't," Asher said. He pointed to the counter behind him. "I'll get you your drink."

"My drink?" He knew her drink? Or was he asking me what I wanted? Suddenly I remembered my tote with my money was still in the break room. I couldn't very well go get it. I patted my pockets, the universal sign for *I forgot my wallet*.

"I got you."

I hated owing anyone anything, but if this were a date, Gemma would've probably accepted, right? "Okay . . . thank you."

He left without another word, so he must've known her drink. I hoped it was good. I was kind of picky . . . really picky, plus I had lactose issues. Kamala knew that. She'd make my actual drink. I tried to catch her eye, but she was already talking to Asher. I slowly sat down.

"So," Dale said. "Gemma . . ."

"Yes . . ."

"What happened to the red rose?"

Was he speaking in code? My face must've shown my confusion because he continued, "From your garden? You were supposed to be carrying one so he'd know it was you."

She was going to carry a rose? Who did this faker think she

was? Audrey Hepburn? Also, didn't he ask Asher ten minutes ago how he would know it was her? Was he messing with me? I could give it right back. "I woke up this morning and they were all dead."

His eyebrows popped up. "All of them?"

"Every last one."

"Huh. Bad luck. Some might've taken that as a sign."

"I don't believe in signs." My mom thought everything was a sign. If two bugs splattered on our windshield at the exact same moment on the highway, that meant, she used to insist, that we were supposed to take the next exit. Something might be waiting for us. There never was, but that didn't stop her from pretending the first seedy gas station we came to had something we were supposed to buy or someone we were supposed to talk to.

"So what's your deal?" Dale said.

"My deal?"

He gestured toward my face. "What's a girl like you doing talking to a nerd like Asher?"

"I like nerds." That was true. But was Asher really a nerd? And what kind of nerd? The fandom kind or the math-whiz kind? "And what kind of girl do you think I am?"

"Familiar," Dale said suddenly.

"What?" I asked, my attention now fully on him. His eyes were still assessing me.

"I've seen you somewhere before."

"I don't think so." I hadn't recognized them when they came in, meaning they probably went to a different high school. And neither of them had seen me when they walked in the café. Were they better at hiding their notice than I'd given them credit for?

Asher plopped onto the bench seat next to me, causing the bench seat to bounce. He laughed and I couldn't help but smile. "Sorry," he said. "I have more power than I thought."

"You really do," I said. The exchange sounded like something from one of those inspirational posters.

"Here's your drink." He slid it in front of me.

"Thank you," I said.

"I can't believe you're really here," he said. "After all this time."

"Two months," Dale said. "It's only been two months."

Good. I could work with two months. There's no way she'd given too many details about herself in that amount of time. Especially because she was probably making half the things up. That's what catfish did, right? They created fake people.

"It feels like at least two and a *half* months," Asher said, a teasing twinkle in his eyes. His hand inched toward mine on the bench and before I knew it, he'd linked pinkies with me, which was actually quite adorable.

I picked up the hot drink in front of me and took a sip.

"The animal shelter!" Dale said loudly. "You work there."

The taste of black coffee with loads of vanilla creamer, definitely not *my* drink, filled my mouth at the same moment I processed Dale's very correct statement. I saved myself from spitting the mouthful of coffee across the table but did not save myself from sucking half of it into my lungs, resulting in a spastic coughing fit.

Asher patted my back as my eyes watered uncontrollably. After several agonizing minutes I finally cleared my airway.

"You okay?" Asher asked for at least the fifth time.

I nodded, grabbed a napkin from the holder in the middle

of the table, and patted beneath my eyes. "It was hot. The drink was hot."

"I'm sorry," he said.

"It wasn't your fault." It was actually Kamala's fault. She gave her bestie Gemma's drink. Probably to prove a point. I crumpled the napkin and set it on the table, shooting Kamala a look. She was either ignoring me or pretending to.

"You do, right?" Dale said, undeterred by my near-death experience. "Work at the animal shelter."

"She doesn't—" Asher started at the same exact moment I said, "Yes." Because I did. I worked at the animal shelter, Petsacular. Had for over a year.

"You didn't tell me that," Asher said.

"Then you would've come and found me before I was ready to meet you," I said, thinking fast.

A shy smile lifted one corner of his mouth. "Probably true."

"Who did you adopt?" I asked Dale.

"My sister adopted a scraggly orange-and-white cat."

Scraggly? Did he only like purebreds or something? "Chuck Norris?"

He scoffed as if the name didn't fit. "Yes."

"Did she change his name?" I asked.

"She mostly calls him Norris."

"Nice," I said. I was going to win over Asher's friend. Wait, why did I care if I won him over? He was kind of a punk. Plus, I wasn't really Gemma. She was a catfish who had been lying to Asher. It wasn't like I was going to permanently take her place. I was just trying to help him save face, make it so he didn't have to perform

16

some crazy dare for his entire school, and most likely the entire internet, to see.

"Petsacular," Asher said. "Right there, this whole time."

"Did you think I lived in the internet signal or something?"

"My phone screen," he said, giving my sarcasm right back.

A smile crept onto my face. It always made me happy when a guy could fire back. "Fair."

"But really, I couldn't picture you roaming around our town anywhere. Now I can."

"Now you can." I needed his friend to leave so I could tell Asher the truth.

"Doesn't the name of the pet shelter drive you crazy?" he said, thoughtfully. "It's always driven me crazy. So close to being an—"

"Anagram," I interrupted him.

"Exactly," he said.

"Yes! It drives me crazy. I tried to tell Kam—uh—one of my friends, but she didn't care."

Kamala cough-laughed across the room. She wasn't ignoring me after all.

"How could they add one more *c* to that word, though?" Asher said. "They really can't. It's tragic."

"It's totally tragic," I said. "They shouldn't have used the name at all. There are so many other wordplays that wouldn't be so maddening. Paws Here, for example."

He smiled. "Fur-ever Friends."

"Catitude."

"Ooh, that's a good one," he said.

"It's true, I should name animal shelters for a living."

"It does take a very specific set of skills," Asher said.

I laughed.

"What are you two talking about?" Dale asked before we could go on.

"Petsacular," I said, and when he gave me a blank stare, I added, "A rearranged version of *spectacular.* Well, one letter short."

"It's just wordplay," he said. "It's not supposed to be an anagram."

"But it should've been," Asher said.

"It's too close," I said, and we both laughed.

"So you're a nerd too," Dale said with a nod, as if finally understanding why I had been talking to Asher. Well . . . why he *thought* I had been talking to Asher.

"I told you she was," Asher said.

"So why didn't you send a real picture?" Dale asked. Why was he trying so hard to prove Asher had been fooled? Couldn't he just accept this new reality and move on?

"Connection shouldn't be about looks," I said.

"You were testing him?" Dale asked. I really wished he'd leave. He was taking the fun out of this. Although once he left it wouldn't be fun either. I'd have to tell Asher the truth, and that goofy grin he had on his face would be gone. But I'd have done him a favor. It was for the best. It would save him from a night of humiliation and being more hurt in the future.

Time seemed to go both fast and slow as I sat there, dodging specific questions, trying to keep answers vague, and pretending to drink coffee all at the same time. This was too much thinking for summer vacation, and further proof that spontaneity was overrated.

Just when I started to wonder how much longer I could keep this up, Dale stood suddenly. "It's time."

"It's time? Already?" Asher asked.

"Time for what?" I said.

"We have to go," Asher said. "Dale's family has this dinner party tonight. Hey, maybe you—"

"Can call him later," Dale said, obviously not wanting Asher to extend me any sort of invite.

Asher gave me a grimace. "I'll talk to you later, yeah?"

"Do you have to leave right now?" I asked. "Can't *you* stay for a little longer?"

Dale once again interrupted with "You were late."

"I'm sorry," Asher said, giving my hand a quick squeeze before standing up himself. "Next time."

There wouldn't be a next time. "Can he go without you?" I asked, softer this time, while giving him a pleading look that I hoped he couldn't resist.

"I drove," Asher said, dashing my hopes.

"Right." I stood up and followed Asher out of the booth and to the worn wood floor just in front of the door.

"Thanks," he said, giving me another one of his world-class hugs. "For showing. You're . . . amazing." He whispered that last word.

I sank against him, holding him tight right back. When was the last time I had a hug like this from a guy? Phillip? Last year? No, Phillip wasn't really a hugger. He'd always just wanted to make out. Maybe that was why I didn't even cry when we went our separate ways. Kamala said it was because I never let anyone in, had too many rules, but what did she know? She'd obviously never been hugged like this either.

"Gemma," Asher said, for what I assumed wasn't the first time. "Are you okay?"

"What?" I let go and took a step back. "Yes, I'm fine. It was good to finally meet you."

"I'll DM you later."

"Oh yeah, for sure. Bye."

He gave me his goofy smile and then they were gone. I watched them through the ocean-painted window as they left and climbed into a blue car parked out front. Then they drove away.

I could feel Kamala behind me before I saw her.

"What are you going to do now? You just made that boy fall in love with you."

CHAPTER 3

• • • • • • • • • • • • • •

Rule: *If he doesn't exist online he can't exist*
in your heart.

"He's not in love with me. He's in love with Gemma," I said, turning to face her.

"Who is most likely some forty-year-old man."

"Ew."

The man who had come in earlier was sipping on his coffee while looking at books in the corner nook. I lowered my voice and whispered, "Ew," again. "Maybe this Gemma person is real and just . . . shy."

Kamala blew air through her lips. "Oh, okay. *Now* you're changing your story?" She pointed to the back hall. "What happened to all that *oh, she's totally fake* talk?"

"Apparently I'm hug starved." I kicked at the blue-and-white checkered tile floor.

"What?"

"Nothing."

"No, what?" she asked.

"That boy can hug, is all. I'm rooting for him."

She put her hands on her hips. "Wait, do *you* like *him*?"

"Stop, I just met him." Which was the first of many strikes against him. "You know I like Chad." Well, I was *on my way* to liking Chad. I worked with him at Petsacular and so far, he was meeting most of my criteria. The list Kamala said was an impossible set of standards. Chad would prove her wrong.

"Oh, right, Chad. You haven't said his name in a while. I figured you decided he wasn't right for you."

"Slow and steady, Kami."

She chuckled. "And the perfect hugger?" she said, nodding toward the corner booth.

"He was nice. Like I said, I hope his catfish is real." My eyes flitted to the table where my mostly full, now-cold coffee still sat. I pointed. "Did you poison me with dairy?"

She covered her face. "I'm sorry! He stood there and watched me make it, like he wanted me to get it just right. I thought you'd taste it and know not to drink any more."

"I knew it was too good to be dairy-free." I hoped I hadn't drunk enough to regret it later.

Kamala patted my stomach. "I'm sorry, Wren's stomach. Be nice to her."

I swatted her hands away. "Don't be weird."

She laughed.

I glanced back toward the register, my eyes zeroing in on the small wooden box on the counter. I looked at Kamala, then back at the box.

"Don't even think about it," she said, and we both took off running toward the counter. I reached it first, but she was right behind me, her hands slamming over mine before I could open the box. "This is private café business."

"Whatever, you read them to me all the time."

She sighed. "Fine, but let me open it."

I stepped back and lifted my hands in surrender. She opened the lid, revealing the one and only folded piece of paper inside at the moment. She took it out and dramatically unfolded it, then read, "Have it your way."

"Have it your way?" I asked. "That's what Asher wrote?"

She flipped the paper over, looked at the back, which was obviously blank, then held it up for me to see.

" 'Have it your way,' " I read out loud. "What does that mean?"

She crumpled up the paper and dropped it in the trash can by the counter. "Who knows? At least it wasn't a complaint."

By the time Kamala got off work and we watched a very unromantic sunset (not a single cloud to paint the sky) it was almost eight o'clock. My dad's car was in the driveway as I pulled up to my house. He would have gotten home about thirty minutes ago. He'd have come inside, hung his car keys on the hook to the right of the door, sat on the bench to the left of the door and unlaced his shoes. He would have put them carefully underneath the bench. Then he had gone to the sink, washed his hands (which he'd already washed before leaving work but that he somehow thought he could get cleaner). They wouldn't get cleaner; he was a mechanic, they were permanently lined black. Next he'd watch about thirty minutes of television and finally, he'd go take a shower.

I may have liked a well-planned day, but Dad had fallen into a rut of predictability. It wasn't a plan, it was just his habits, repeated over and over again. I wasn't even sure if he realized how predictable he was.

I let myself in the front door. My dad was sitting on the couch watching some nature show.

"Hi," I said, adding my keys to the hook next to my dad's.

"Hey, Bird. How was your day?" He was sitting on the edge of the couch, like he did before his shower, worried his coveralls were going to dirty the cushions. The couch was too big for the cramped living room, but it was in good shape, so he would not buy a new one anytime soon.

"Eh, kind of boring. But I did watch a very unromantic sunset."

"You had a date?" he asked.

"With Kamala."

He smiled. "How is Kamala?"

I leaned against the back of the couch and watched a tiger on the television stalk a deer. "She's still way nicer than me."

"I doubt that," he said, like dads are required to.

"How was *your* day?" I asked. Dad worked for a guy named Niles who I hated more than I hated almost anyone. He overworked my dad but didn't pay him like he overworked him. For years Dad had talked about opening his own small mechanic shop, but he never had the time or money to fulfill that dream and eventually he stopped talking about it. And that was the main reason I hated Niles. He was a dream killer.

"Same old, same old."

"You should tell Niles that you have a life outside of work," I said.

"Do I? Have a life?"

I gasped in fake offense. "You live and die for me, Dad."

"Do I do both at the same time?"

I crinkled my nose. "That's not the saying, is it? You live and breathe for me?"

"I definitely do that." He clicked off the television. "I'm going to—"

"Shower?" I finished for him.

"Yes," he said.

"I'll make some dinner."

"Thanks," he said.

"Is Zoey here?" Zoey was my older sister. She had moved out a year ago with some friends, but she dropped by often.

"No," he said.

"Okay, dinner for two."

He headed for his room and I went to the kitchen. The fridge was basically empty. Tomorrow was one of my days off work and, by default, grocery day. In the pantry I found a pack of spaghetti and a jar of sauce, so I started some water boiling.

Twenty minutes later, my dad came downstairs, hair wet from a shower, wearing flannel pajama bottoms and a T-shirt. He was broad-shouldered, with short salt-and-pepper hair and kind brown eyes that always looked tired. We looked nothing alike. I looked almost exactly like my mom in photos I'd seen of her at my age: tall with long brown hair and judgy blue eyes. When I was twelve, I chopped all my hair off because of the similarities between us. Kamala's mom had to fix my kitchen-scissor massacre. I feared that the impulse to cut all my hair off actually made me more like my mom than the long hair ever did. It's been long ever since.

"I need to shop," I said when my dad looked at the plate of spaghetti and canned green beans on the table.

"No, this is good. Thank you."

"You know, I bet if you owned your own place your boss would let you go home before seven o'clock at night."

"I have a feeling my boss would be a hardnose."

I smiled. "True, he *is* kind of uptight."

"Do you have fifty grand I can borrow?" he asked.

"I hear the bank lets people borrow money, but I might be wrong."

He pushed the green beans around his plate before saying, "Yeah, I should look into that."

He wouldn't. My dad wasn't a risk-taker. He was safe, predictable.

"Well, I should go to bed." And by bed, I meant binge a show on my laptop for a couple of hours.

"Good night," he said. "Oh, and your mom wants to call this week."

"Yeah, sure," I said.

I didn't want to talk to my mother. She'd walked out on us seven years ago and never looked back. Since then, she'd been a string of unfulfilled promises. Well, technically even before she walked out she'd built up a nice habit of not following through on her word, of living from moment to moment, spontaneous and impulsive. But leaving pretty much sealed the deal. And so, for my own sanity, I'd put up some boundaries. Talking to her when I wanted to was one of those. But my dad didn't need to know all that. He already worried enough.

"He's rich," I said, turning my phone toward Kamala. We were sitting in her living room, windows open, fans blowing, watching television. It didn't get hot often on the central coast. The Pacific Ocean, our very own climate controller, made every day mostly the same. But several weeks during the summer, when the breezes died down and the sun beat heavy, I longed for air conditioners to be standard like they were in other places. Today was one of those days.

"Who's rich?" she asked, looking at my phone. "Is that . . . ?"

"Dale."

"Are you cyberstalking him?"

"I've been trying to find Asher for the last couple of days. I was hoping to message him and tell him I'm not really Gemma. But he doesn't exist online." Between chores and work and a proper trip to the beach, I hadn't spent much time looking, but the searching I *had* done led to nothing. "You know people without social media are suspicious."

She gasped. "You are practically nonexistent online!"

"I know! And I'm *very* suspicious. Not to be trusted at all. You should add the social media rule to *your* love list."

"I don't have a love list. You make enough rules for the both of us."

I gave a sitting bow. "You're welcome."

Kamala smiled, then took my phone and started scrolling down Dale's page full of pictures of him on boats and in big houses and traveling to exotic places. The guy was loaded.

"Is it wrong that I now find him more attractive?" she asked.

I shoved her shoulder with a laugh.

She showed me a picture of him in a pair of short swim trunks, shirtless. "I mean . . ." She waggled her eyebrows.

"Too bad he's a huge jerk."

She rolled her eyes. "*Huge* jerk? He was just trying to protect his friend."

"By threatening to humiliate him?"

"I mean, maybe Asher wasn't listening. Maybe that's all Dale had left to get through to him."

"You're defending him?" I asked.

"He seemed harmless to me."

I grabbed my phone back. "It doesn't matter. He's not the one I want to message. He's the one who can't know what I did or he will definitely follow through with his original plan."

"You could look through all of Dale's followers. Asher *has* to be online. He was getting catfished, after all, which is pretty much only possible through social media. Maybe he goes by a weird name or something."

"Ugh. I don't care enough. I'm just curious if Gemma ever

fessed up. But if I have to put in actual work? Not worth it." I dropped my phone next to me and turned toward the fan. "It's so hot! Let's go get Popsicles or sit in a freezer or something."

I stood and pulled Kamala to her feet.

"I now know someone with a boat," she hummed. "We should ask him if we can go for a ride. Pretty sure a whale can't swallow a speedboat whether it's trying to or not."

"Funny. And you better not be talking about Dale."

She laughed as we headed for the door. "No, but really. Do you think he'd take us on his boat?"

CHAPTER 4

. . . .

*Rule: Never date a guy who has bad taste
in friends.*

Despite its unfortunate name, Petsacular was one of my very favorite places to be. And as I stood, earbuds in, hosing down a recently vacated kennel, I smiled at my good fortune in landing this job. A lot of the people who worked here were volunteers, but I actually got paid to cuddle, walk, and bathe animals.

As I watched the foamy brownish-yellow liquid head toward the drain, the water coming from the hose in my hand drizzled to a stop. I turned around to see Erin, my boss, standing by the faucet and pointing at her ears. She'd obviously been trying to get my attention.

I plucked out my earbuds. "Sorry!"

"It's okay. You have a visitor up front."

"An appointment? Did they say who they're here to see?"

"You," she said as I walked closer.

"No, which animal? Please say Bean. I've been posting about him a lot." Bean was a brown pit bull mix with little white tufts of fur on each paw who I also called Beanie and Beano and Beanster and Goodest Boy and a number of other endearments. He'd been at the shelter the longest—nine months. Two hundred seventy-four days, to be exact—it was written on the whiteboard in the break room. Maybe that was why I felt so connected to him—because I knew him the best. Or maybe it was because I knew how it felt not to be chosen.

"I'm not sure," Erin said.

"Hey, Good Boy," I said as I passed Bean's kennel. He gave a single bark. "Cross your toes that this one's for you." I knelt down by the chain-link door and put my palm against it. His tail was wagging his whole backside as he licked my hand through the door, then finished with another bark. "Yes, you're such a good boy. So handsome and smart."

"Only for you," Erin mumbled.

"That's not true. Don't listen to her, you love everyone, don't you, boy?"

"He really doesn't. He refused to walk for Rodrigo yesterday, made him carry him from the back play area. That's why he has the longest-resident award."

I turned back to Bean. "Just because you're particular doesn't mean you're not lovable."

"That sounds like someone else I know," Erin teased.

"No, I'm both particular *and* not lovable," I joked back.

She laughed.

I stood and crossed my fingers as I passed more kennels full of barking dogs. I pushed through the swinging door to the front lobby, used the hand sanitizer attached to the wall, and rounded the corner.

An older woman I knew I should've recognized but didn't stood with a smile. "Wren!" she said.

"Hi, nice to see you again."

"I've come back for Toto. I couldn't stop thinking about her."

"Oh . . ." Oh! The woman had been here before. "Toto found a home already."

"What? You said you'd hold her for two weeks."

There was no way I said that. We had animals to move here, this wasn't some furniture storage facility. "Did you put a deposit down? Or fill out paperwork?"

The woman wasn't smiling anymore. "No, but I told you I liked her a lot."

I tilted my head, assessing her for a moment. "Can I introduce you to one of my very favorite dogs in the shelter?"

The woman looked at the tall counter where we didn't have anyone working at the moment. We were short-staffed today. Then she gave a reluctant grunt that I took as an agreement.

"Follow me," I said.

We passed several rows of kennels before we came to Bean's. I presented him like the prize he was. The woman glanced into his kennel. "I don't know about a pit."

"He's the sweetest. Aren't you, Bean?"

Bean took one look at the lady, snorted in her direction, then retreated to the far corner of the kennel.

"Bean, come here."

He turned his backside to her.

The woman gasped. "Well, that is the rudest dog I've ever met."

Okay, so maybe Bean wasn't the best introduction to make. Erin was right, he *was* a little particular. Or a lot.

"I really just want Toto," she said. "Can you call the person you gave her to and explain the situation?"

"What situation?"

"That she was mine."

My eyes went wide and I held back a grunt. "I'm sorry, but she wasn't yours. She has a family now. A little girl adopted her." I nearly finished with: *Guess you'll fill out paperwork next time.* I stopped myself, biting down on my tongue and taking a deep breath. I did not say everything that came into my mind.

Regardless, the woman huffed out, "Is your manager here?"

This time I let out a heavy sigh. Why were people so annoying sometimes? "Yes, if you'll wait in the lobby, I'll get her for you."

The woman headed off, not giving a single glance to any of the dogs she passed.

"I'm sorry I tried to give you to her, Bean. We can do much better than that."

He gave me a whimper and lay down on his cot.

I found Erin in the vaccination room with some bunnies. My mood was immediately lifted. "Oh wow, look at these little cuties. When did they come in?"

"Yesterday."

"They are adorable." I scratched the soft fur between the ears of a brown bunny.

"I swear I don't know how you don't take home every animal in this place."

"My dad won't let me." Mainly because animals cost money and we already struggled with that. But he also claimed allergies that he'd yet to prove. "Oh! That lady out front who asked for me? She wants to talk to you now because I gave her dog to someone else."

"You did?"

"No, she couldn't make up her mind and left. That was two weeks ago."

Erin curled her lip. "I don't want to deal with that."

"I know. But that's why they pay you the big bucks."

She scoffed because we both knew that wasn't true. She tucked the bunny she was holding into a plastic carrier and left the room. I followed her so I could eavesdrop in case I needed to provide my side of the story.

Before she reached the front lobby Erin turned and said, "We got three new intakes today. I put them in kennel C. Will you help Chad assess them?"

"Chad's here?" I asked. How had I missed him?

"Just arrived," she said.

I smiled. It had been a week since we'd worked together. "Yes, I can help him."

Chad was in the kennel as I approached, squatting in front of one of the new dogs, a corgi mix with white eyebrows and over-sized ears. He was clipping her into a leash. His dark hair was long, halfway down his collar, and his shoulders were wide under his Petsacular T-shirt. But I didn't like him because he was hot. In fact, that was a rule on my list: *You can't like someone just because they're hot, Wren. No, really, stop it.* I liked him because he was smart and patient and hardworking.

I threaded my fingers through the chain link of the gate. "Hey, I'm supposed to help assess the new dogs." I cleared my throat. My voice had sounded huskier than I meant it to.

Chad pivoted in his squat and looked up at me, a half smile coming onto his handsome face. Seriously, his jaw could cut glass. "Hey, yeah, there are three, so I could use the help. Will you grab two more leads?" He pointed to the wall next to me.

I took two leashes off the hook and passed them to him. He expertly restrained the remaining dogs, despite their squirminess.

"Did they come in together?" I asked. New dogs usually had their own kennels unless they were dropped off together.

"I guess their owner passed away suddenly."

"And they probably didn't even get to go to the funeral."

"They didn't." He opened the gate, handed the corgi off to me, and led the way outside.

"No, it was . . . a joke." *Wren, nobody gets your dark humor.* The dog, nipping at my heels as we walked, was medium-sized and butterscotch with short little legs that pedaled along at a slow pace.

I stopped, looked down at the creature, and said, "It's not polite to herd me." She looked up and tilted her head. "Are you going to behave? Do you know any commands? Sit." She tilted her head again. "No?"

"You coming? Or do you need a moment with the dog?" Chad asked over his shoulder when he got to the door leading out back.

"You think I need alone time with the dog? I'm not flirting with her," I said.

He rolled his eyes. "That's not what I meant."

"Is that how girls flirt with you? Tell you to sit and behave?" He obviously hadn't been picking up on *my* way of flirting.

"Um . . . no." He pushed through the door.

I proceeded after him. "I was kidding."

"I know, it was funny," he said, but I wasn't sure he meant it. Not on my love list: *Your potential suitor must think you are hilarious.* I wondered for a moment if I should add it, but Chad's handsome face shook that bit of vanity right out of me.

I let the door swing shut behind us.

The back of the shelter was amazing. There was a big grassy area with benches and ramps and tunnels where people could come and play with the animals. There was a walking path and a fountain. There was even a mini house, a one-room structure made to look like a living room, where the animals could practice their indoor manners. And in the far back corner of the space was a penned-in area where we took new dogs, ones we were assessing, to make sure they passed behavior tests before we introduced them to other dogs or potential adopters.

Chad unhooked the latch on the gate to the pen.

"Do they have names?" I asked, the big-eared old lady nipping at my heels again.

Chad cringed. "Probably. I forgot to look."

"Did you notice if they came from an English-speaking home?"

"What do you mean?" Chad asked, tugging on the leashes of the dogs, who had taken to sniffing every square inch of grass they could right outside the gate.

"They're older. If they've been spoken to in a different language their whole lives, that might help us now. You know?"

"That's true."

"Do you know the Spanish word for *sit*?" I asked.

"I don't."

Do you know the Spanish words for *Do you want to grab coffee after work?* That's what I should've said but it felt too forced. Plus, I had no idea, none whatsoever, how Chad would react to that. And knowing how something was going to play out was important to me. I needed a subtler plan. Something I could explain away if he seemed uninterested. I pulled out my phone and went to Google Translate. "I learned how to say *sit* in Spanish a couple of months ago for the golden retriever, Bella, who was in here, but I forgot it."

"I remember Bella. She was sweet."

"She was."

"Gemma!" The name didn't register with me at first. It was being yelled from the grassy area behind us and I was waiting for my phone, the little wheel in the corner spinning, to provide my translation. The internet at the shelter sucked.

The dog had walked around my legs once and was now chewing on my shoelace.

"No, no," I said, shaking my foot a bit.

Chad was in the pen taking his dogs off leash. He glanced up at me, his dark hair brushing his jawline.

"What's your favorite place to get coffee? Maybe we could go after work." The words came out fast and all at once, surprising me. I'd done it. I'd actually done it. The swelling pride I felt was quickly masked by panic as Chad's expression turned to surprise, or more accurately, horror.

"I . . . ," Chad started. "It's just I don't really think that's a good . . ." He rubbed at the bridge of his nose like something stunk. He was disgusted at the idea of going out with me?

How could I save this? Take it back? My cheeks were heating up, my breath hitching.

"Gemma!"

My brain seemed to jump-start along with my heart. I gasped and spun around to see Asher waving enthusiastically at me. I took a step forward and immediately tripped over the leash.

I caught myself with my palms before face-planting onto the grass. One hand landed in a small puddle that I assumed was pee, because most small puddles here were. Also, because it smelled exactly like dog pee. I curled my nose and glared at my short-legged companion, who was now sitting like a good girl, her tongue hanging out, making her look like she was smiling.

"You think this is funny?" I asked her under my breath. "I bet you do."

"Are you okay?" Asher asked, rushing forward.

"Apparently, I forgot how leashes worked," I said.

"The leash seemed to work well. Your legs, not so much."

I let out a single laugh. "I'm still on the ground. Your jokes are unwelcome."

He held out his hand. "I'm sorry. Are you hurt?"

"I'm fine." I didn't take his hand because of the dog pee situation. I pushed myself to standing, passed the dog off to Chad, and shook off my wet hand. Luckily, sanitizing wet wipes were at nearly every station here and I freed several from the stand by the gate, scrubbing at my hand while Asher stood and watched, his expression guilt-ridden.

I offered him a smile as I threw the wipes in the trash. "Hi." I opened my mouth to form some sort of apology or at least an explanation about tricking him at the café, when it hit me: he had been yelling the name Gemma. What did that mean? He still didn't know I wasn't her?

"Hi," he returned.

Chad gave a command to one of the dogs in the pen, reminding me that tripping was the least embarrassing thing that had happened to me in the last five minutes. That's when my brain came up with a stupid solution. I'd saved Asher from humiliation in the coffee shop and he was going to save me now, even if he didn't realize it.

"I didn't know you were coming," I spit out. "Did you get the DM I sent you just now about getting coffee after work?" I bit my lip and let my eyes flit to Chad. He tilted his head as if analyzing our conversation.

"No, I left my phone in the car. But yes, that sounds like fun."

"Awesome." I hoped Chad was buying this new narrative, and I added this lie to the list of lies I'd have to confess to Asher later.

"Dale!" Asher called. "I found her!" He looked over his shoulder and I followed his gaze to see Dale balancing on top of one of the tunnels in the doggie play area.

"What are you guys doing here?" I asked.

"We came to see you."

Had his catfish really not fessed up? Had he been in contact with her at all since the café?

"When do you get off?" Asher asked.

I checked the time on my phone. "About an hour and a half?"

39

Dale, now down from his perch, had his phone out and was panning it slowly back and forth as he walked our way.

Asher jerked his thumb in Dale's direction. "We can hang around until then. Do you need extra volunteers today? I'm an excellent dog walker. I know how leashes work and everything."

"You're a brat," I said with a laugh.

"You should have him walk Bean," Chad said, tossing a tennis ball. All three dogs just watched it bounce off the chain-link fence, not interested in retrieving it at all.

"I'll walk whoever," Asher said. "Just tell me what to do."

There was no way I was making him walk Bean. That dog would turn him off all dogs. He was too difficult. "You need to talk to our volunteer coordinator and fill out paperwork."

"What she means is that you'll need to sign something that says if Bean bites you, you won't sue," Chad said. Why was there suddenly an edge to Chad's voice? That was new.

"Bean won't bite him," I said. Bean may have been difficult, but he wasn't aggressive.

Dale stood by the pen, aiming his camera at the three new intakes. "They look like little old men," he said. "Do people actually adopt dogs that are on death's door?"

I opened my mouth but immediately shut it again, holding back a snarky response.

Chad said, "Yes, they do."

Dale shrugged and swung toward me, his phone pointed at my green polo shirt.

"What are you doing?" I asked, covering my chest.

Asher pushed Dale's arm down, forcing him to lower the phone. "Dude."

"Your name is Wren?" Dale asked, and I realized his camera must've been on the name tag I hadn't thought about until that moment.

CHAPTER 5

· · · · · · · · · · · · · · ·

Rule: *Never date a guy who makes you feel*
out of control.

I thought it was over. That after seeing my name tag, learning my
actual name, Asher would finally put two and two together and
figure out I wasn't the girl he'd been talking to.

But before I could say a word, he'd said, "Of course you
wouldn't go by your real name online. With a name like Wren, you
probably figured I'd be able to look you up." He had given me the
same excuse I'd used for not telling him where I worked.

I'd half-heartedly agreed as Dale listened, his eyes narrowed in
suspicion.

After that, I'd sent Asher and Dale off to see Rodrigo, the volunteer coordinator, and I hadn't seen them since.

That was an hour ago.

In that time, Chad and I had both avoided talking about anything beyond the dogs in the pen. I was too scared to let him finish
rejecting me. It was better to pretend it hadn't happened.

"We need to introduce another dog," I said to Chad, glancing around. "These dogs obviously came together. We need to see how they'll do with an unfamiliar friend."

"Tomorrow," Chad said. "They've had enough activity for the day."

He was right. We didn't want to introduce them already worn out from playing. I nodded and gathered the leads by the gate.

"Who were those guys earlier?" Chad asked, taking the leashes I offered.

I guess we weren't going to pretend. I swallowed. "Um . . . just a guy . . . I'm . . ." My brain flashed to the look of disgust Chad had earlier when he thought I was asking him out. "Dating."

"You're dating a guy who didn't know your real name?" He squatted and hooked a leash to the nearest collar.

I joined him, clipping one as well. "We met online. I don't give my real name online."

He nodded like that made perfect sense. "I didn't know you were dating anyone."

"Yeah . . ." *I didn't know either.* "I mean, just barely." As in, an hour ago.

"Earlier, I thought you were . . ." He trailed off.

"You thought I was what?" I asked innocently.

He stood and wiped his hands on the back of his jeans. "I thought we were . . ."

Was he going to finish a sentence? Had I read the situation wrong? Did he actually like me? Had I screwed everything up? It was too late to take back my fake dating situation now.

"What about you?" I asked when he didn't finish. I tugged on the leash I held, moving toward the gate. "Are you seeing anyone?"

He followed me. "No. And I don't usually date girls I work with."

Was that what he was going to say before? I held back a groan.

"It's one of my rules," he continued.

"You have rules?"

"Doesn't everyone?"

"If there were no rules, how could we break them?" I joked, and opened the gate.

He stepped through with his dogs. "I don't break my rules."

"No. Me neither." It was a joke. Good thing I hadn't added that rule about thinking I was funny.

"Usually," Chad added, confusing me and giving me hope at the same time.

My short-legged friend was too tired to herd me this time as we walked toward the main building. "Good girl," I cooed in her direction.

"Not sure she's earned that title yet," Chad said. He was frustrated that none of the dogs responded to any of his commands, in English or Spanish.

I nudged Chad with my elbow playfully. "She has."

Chad held the door open for me, letting the echoing barks out into the open air.

We rounded the corner and I saw Rodrigo walking our way. Slightly behind him, Asher was holding a leash. I followed the line of that leash until my eyes collided with a dog—Bean. I gave an audible gasp.

"Check it out, Wren," Rodrigo called. "Look who your mini-me likes. Are you jealous?"

Asher waved at me and then he and Rodrigo stopped in front of Bean's kennel. Behind me, Chad was opening kennel C.

"Wren, the dog," he was saying.

"Oh, right." I absently handed him the leash and watched as Asher squatted down, rubbed Bean's head, scratched behind his ears, and then led him through the kennel door that Rodrigo was holding open.

Chad had put away the dogs we'd been working with and was now standing beside me. "Is that Bean?" he asked. "I had been kidding about the whole walking-him thing."

"Yeah, it is."

"He likes your boyfriend," Chad said.

Asher exited the kennel and headed our way. His big smile was on and his auburn hair was flopping in his eyes. I didn't remember what color his eyes were but I found myself wanting to know. His lanky limbs were relaxed, his gait assured.

"He's not my boy—" I started, but when Asher reached me, he wrapped me up in a hug.

I melted against him. I had forgotten how good of a hugger he was, but was being reminded all over again as his hands pressed against my lower back. "You walked Bean?" I said into his shoulder.

"Was I not supposed to?"

I looked up at him. His eyes were a brownish green—hazel. "Those are my favorite," I said.

He smirked. "What?"

"I . . . Nothing." I took a step back, out of his arms, and tried to shake off this feeling, whatever it was. The feeling of being just a little out of control. I didn't like it. "This is Chad. Chad, this is Asher."

"Hey," Chad said. "Wren, I'll write today's report on the dogs. You get tomorrow's."

"Sure," I responded.

After Chad left, Asher said, "I talked to Rodrigo about changing the name of the shelter. He was sympathetic to our concerns."

I laughed. "You did not."

"I really wanted to," he said.

"Rodrigo doesn't wield that kind of power."

"I figured."

"Where's Dale?" I asked.

"They assigned him to check-in."

That didn't surprise me. There had been nobody up front earlier. It was a boring job that consisted of making visitors sign in, giving them a squirt of sanitizer, and telling them someone would be right with them.

"You almost off?" Asher asked.

"Another thirty minutes," I said. "Do you have to . . . ? Are your . . . ?" I knew nothing about Asher, but my online counterpart did and if I asked him the wrong question now, he'd know we weren't the same person. *That's a good thing, Wren. He needs to know.*

"My parents won't care," he filled in for me.

"Right. Cool."

"I do have to grab my brother at five, though, so maybe you can do that with us before we get that coffee?"

Right, I had asked him out for coffee. "With you and Dale? You drove together?" *Again?*

"Yes, we did. Dale doesn't . . . well, you know."

I had no idea. Didn't what? Get his hands dirty? "Right."

Erin walked briskly by the row where Asher and I stood and then was gone.

"That's my boss." I rushed after her, Asher followed. "Erin!" I called out as she reached the door to the medical room.

She turned around, but I couldn't read her expression.

"How did it go with the customer?"

"She was mad. I told her she'd be the first call if we received a similar dog in the future."

"Sorry I couldn't calm her down," I said.

Erin smiled. "It's okay. I think you like animals more than people sometimes."

"Most of the time," I assured her.

"Some customers are unreasonable. I wouldn't have held a dog for two weeks without a deposit and paperwork either." Her gaze turned to Asher. "Are you the famous volunteer?"

"I've only been here an hour, so probably not," Asher said.

"If Bean likes you, you gain renown pretty quick around here," she said.

"Oh, then yes, my picture should be up on the wall by end of day."

Erin laughed. "You should become a regular volunteer. We need someone Thursday afternoons."

"Did Bean just hire me?"

"It doesn't pay anything," she said.

"Same as my last job. I'm in." Just like that. Asher accepted just like that. Impulsive.

Erin chuckled as she let herself into the medical room.

"Are you trying to make everyone around here like you more than they like me?" I asked.

"That's impossible."

I bit the inside of my cheek. He didn't know me. He knew Gemma or someone pretending to be her. Not me.

"What next?" he asked.

"I need to take pics of the new dogs to post on the Instagram page." I headed for kennel C again.

"Sounds fun." As we walked, the backs of our hands brushed. Neither of us widened the distance to prevent it from happening over and over again the entire length of the hall. Dogs barked and our footsteps echoed and I looked up at Asher and he smiled and I thought, *Good thing I'm cutting this boy loose in an hour, because he breaks too many rules. I need rules. I need control.*

CHAPTER 6

· · · · · · · · · · · · · · · ·

Rule: *Rebounds are only good in basketball.*

What do you mean you're in a car with him?! You know nothing about him! This is how people get murdered! Kamala texted in response to the report I'd made to her from the back seat of Asher's Toyota. He and Dale sat in the front. We were on our way to pick up a little brother whose name Gemma probably knew but I didn't.

He filled out the volunteer paperwork. I read over it. I was right, he doesn't go to our school, he goes to Dalton.

Dalton was the private school in town, serving the rich or ultrasmart.

And, I continued to type, *there was a copy of his license. He's seventeen. I know more about him than any Uber driver who's given me a ride.* I had thought this through. I really needed to talk to Asher, tell him who I was, but Dale was his permanent sidekick, it seemed. Riding with Asher felt like a good way to get him alone so we could finally have a real conversation.

The company knows about the Uber drivers!! They do background checks!

Okay, maybe I hadn't thought it through. *Probably true. But Bean liked him. Bean doesn't even like you.*

Bean likes you! That dog is no judge of character.

I laughed. Asher's eyes met mine in the rearview mirror. I averted my gaze. "What are the videos for?" I asked Dale, who was once again recording.

"TikTok," he said. "Are you on TikTok?"

"No." I had been on TikTok at one point but found myself sucked into the black hole of short clips for hours at a time. I knew I would either graduate from high school with decent grades or become one with the TikTok algorithm, so I deleted it from my phone. "You're trying to go viral with videos of car rides?"

"It's this bug." He pointed to the window and a bug I couldn't see from where I sat. "It's been hanging on for the last five minutes. It will get an amazing voice-over and some killer music. Random things like this go viral all the time. Right, Asher?"

"Bugs are big right now," Asher deadpanned. He flipped on the blinker and then turned into the parking lot of the local car wash. A guy in uniform was sitting on the curb and he stood as Asher pulled up alongside him. He looked a little like Asher: auburn hair, freckles across his nose.

"You're late," he said when he opened the back door.

"Sorry, dog photo shoot," Asher said.

"I don't even want to know what that means." He started to climb in and paused when he saw me.

"Brett, this is Gemma . . . I mean Wren. Wren, this is my little brother, Brett."

He didn't look so little. Unlike Asher, he was bulky and well over six feet tall. His legs barely fit behind the passenger seat as he slid inside. "Hey." He nodded my way.

"Hi. You work at Squeaky Clean?"

"No, I just like to wear the uniform. The cut is very flattering."

I smiled. "A stupid question deserves a stupid answer."

"Yes, it does." He finally cracked a smile. Much like their looks, Brett's and Asher's personalities seemed opposite as well. Where Asher was open and happy, Brett seemed somber and sarcastic.

"Don't be mean, Brett," Asher said.

Dale held up his fist to Brett, who bumped it.

"Missing your real driver again today?" Brett asked.

Dale ran a hand through his hair. "The only reason my butt would be sitting on fake leather."

I laughed but nobody else in the car did. *Wait, did Dale have an actual driver?*

"I think it's called pleather," Asher said.

Brett sized me up. "So you're my brother's online girlfriend? We all thought you were fake and that my brother had become desperate in his post-breakup depression."

"We still could be right," Dale said. "Are you fake, Wren?"

"Are you?" I asked. I wondered what the real Gemma was like. Warm? Genuine? Someone who matched up better with Asher's sweet nature, for sure.

"Ouch," Brett said. "She fires back."

"Anyone want food?" Asher asked, perhaps to change the subject, or maybe because we were passing a McDonald's.

"Home. Shower," Brett grunted.

A few minutes later, and not even close to the part of town I thought we were heading to, Asher pulled up in front of an average-sized house—single story, two-car garage, bright blue door. Considering he went to a private school, I was surprised. Asher didn't seem to be the typical Dalton student. Dale, who had not been dropped off, proving his sidekick status, got out of the car first. Brett climbed out next.

Before he walked away, Brett looked back at me. "Glad to know my brother is not as big of a loser as I thought he was."

"Nice to meet you too," I said. Then he shut the door.

Asher put the car in park and turned all the way around. He pushed his glasses up his nose. "That's the first bit of respect my brother has ever given me."

"Yeah, right," I said with a small chuckle.

"No, he wasn't kidding with the loser talk."

"Well, brothers can be pretty annoying, you should ignore him." Once the front door to the house closed, I asked, "Does Dale really have a private driver?"

"I thought I told you that."

"I'm sure you did," I said.

"He's really not as obnoxious as he seems. I promise."

"I don't need any promises." Wow, that sounded cryptic.

It was time to come clean. I pointed to the passenger seat and he nodded. I climbed over the middle console and awkwardly worked my way to sitting, regretting immediately that I didn't just exit the car and enter the front seat the normal way. By the time I settled in, Asher was laughing.

"I'm usually more graceful when I do that," I said.

"I'm sure you are." He gave a thoughtful smile, then gestured toward his house. "Do you want to come in for a bit?"

"I know I said coffee, but actually, I should probably get home. I didn't tell my dad I was going somewhere after work." On Saturdays, he got off at five, to start his routine two hours earlier.

"Your dad?" Asher asked.

Did Gemma not have a dad? Had she had him fake-die in some tragic accident?

Asher turned sideways and reached over, placing his hand on my forearm. "Tell me about him."

"What do you want to know?"

"Everything. You've been so private with family details."

She had? "My dad works a lot."

"And your mom?"

"Left us years ago to be able to do whatever she wants whenever she wants to." I didn't tell people that, especially people I hardly knew. What was it about him that made me want to spill my guts? Whatever it was, it wasn't good. I needed to stop.

"I'm sorry."

I shrugged. "She's not. You definitely shouldn't be."

"I'm sorry anyway." He circled a small freckle on my arm with his finger. "What does your dad do?"

"He's a mechanic. Which means I will never get a new car. He keeps resurrecting the one I have."

Asher stared at the steering wheel for a moment. "My grand-dad bought me this car. My parents couldn't really afford it."

I wondered if his granddad also paid for his school tuition. "Can your granddad buy me a car?"

"I'll ask him."

I smiled. Why was I stalling? Because I *was* a fake, like Dale had accused me of, and I hated that. "I need to tell you something."

"What is it?" Asher asked, looking at me with those innocent hazel eyes.

Why had the girl online kept up the charade after the café? That seemed strange. Maybe they hadn't messaged since the in-person meeting? Maybe she'd managed to avoid specific questions when she realized someone else had shown up? But if that was the case, why hadn't she outed me?

"Who's Chad, by the way?" he asked before I said anything. "He was asking me all sorts of questions before we left."

"He was? Like what?"

"Like how long we'd been dating and if I liked you and if we were exclusive."

My mouth opened in shock and I quickly shut it. "And what did you tell him?"

"I told him we weren't exclusive but I wanted to be."

My heart thudded hard in my chest. *Oh, calm down, heart, he doesn't even know you. He's talking about Gemma.* "He's a coworker. Has been for the last year. What about you? Post-breakup?" I asked, repeating what Brett had said minutes ago. Dale had also said something similar in the café that first day. "Elinor?" That was the name he'd used.

Asher took a deep breath, suddenly interested in looking out the windshield at a large eucalyptus tree. "Did Dale tell you about her?"

Not in the way he thought. "He didn't say a lot."

"We really don't need to talk about my ex."

"Oh, come on. I just told you I was abandoned by my mom. Which one of us is more screwed up here?"

He crinkled his nose, then sighed. "When I met you, I mean online, when we first started talking, I'd just been dumped."

Rebounds are only good in basketball. Never be someone's rebound. I could see that rule flash through my head in my own handwriting and everything. I shook it away. "How long were you together?"

"About a year."

Too long. "I'm sorry."

"No, don't be," he said. "It was long overdue. We weren't right for each other, but being dumped just destroys your confidence, you know?"

I actually didn't know. I hadn't ever been dumped. I'd never made it to the girlfriend stage of a relationship. "Yeah," I said.

"I was feeling like maybe I wasn't right for anyone. And then *we* started talking and slowly I started feeling better. Then we met . . ."

"And I ruined it?" I wasn't exactly known for helping people feel better about themselves.

"What? No. I felt like myself for the first time in a long time. My point is, I'm glad I met you."

I needed to rip off the Band-Aid. This was getting worse by the second. "Asher, I'm not—" There was a loud smacking noise on the window and I jumped and let out a squeal. I turned to see Asher's brother pressing his face against the glass. He had changed clothes and his hair was wet.

"Hey, jerk-off, Mom said you have to take me to In-N-Out!" His voice was muffled through the window.

"I literally asked you if you wanted food on the way home!" Asher yelled back.

"I changed my mind!"

Asher groaned, then rolled down the window. "Fine. Back seat. I need to take Wren to her car anyway."

"You didn't tell him?" Kamala practically yelled at me as we sat on my bed that night.

"I was going to, but he told me this sad story about losing all his confidence. And his brother was making fun of him, and Dale wants him to commit social suicide."

"Are you talking about Dale's birthday party humiliation he wants to inflict on Asher?" she asked, obviously remembering the conversation from the café as well.

"Yes. If Dale digs around and finds out that not only was he catfished originally but now I seem to be catfishing him . . . in a very different and nice way . . . he'll never let him live it down."

Kamala's brows shot down. "Different and nice way?"

"I mean, he's met me and seen me and I'm trying my hardest not to lie to him."

"That's all you're doing!" she said. "Lying to him."

"No, I'm not. He knows where I work. He's met Bean! I told him about my dad's stupid job and my mom. So see! I'm not lying."

"You told him about your mom?" she asked, surprised. I didn't tell anyone anything about my mom unless they already knew she'd left us. I hardly even talked to Kamala about the situation. Why *had* I told him?

She stood suddenly and began pacing the room, her hands twisting around each other. Her bed was lined with stuffed animals that she held or fidgeted with when she was nervous or thinking. My bedroom didn't contain a single stuffed animal—I hated clutter—so I held a pillow in her direction.

She waved it away. "Don't make fun of me. You're the weird one. Who doesn't have something soft to hug?"

"People who don't need hugs," I said.

"Says the girl who found the perfect hugger." She let out a frustrated sigh. "He seems like a really nice guy, Wren."

"He is. And I'm going to tell him. I am. Maybe after I get Dale off the suspicion trail. Then Asher can just say we weren't right for each other or something, not that he was fooled."

"And if he falls for you in the meantime?" she asked, as if guys fell for me on the regular.

"Oh please. He won't. We're so not right for each other." He'd already broken six of my rules and I'd barely known him for a week.

"Do you like him?" Kamala asked. "Is that why you're doing this?"

"No! I just want to help him."

Her worried expression turned into a disappointed one. "So you feel sorry for him? That's even worse."

"It's not worse. That's what good people with big hearts do."

She pointed to me. "Was that a description of you?"

"I may keep it in a cage, but I have the biggest heart in this town."

Kamala, in all her best-friend sincerity, said, "I know you do," which made me laugh because I had been kidding. My heart was pretty shriveled. "It's your brain I have a problem with. You can't control everything, you know."

"I know," I said. But I could control *most* things.

"I'm just worried this is all going to blow up in your face and he's going to get hurt."

"I won't hurt him. It's Dale who wants to make a fool of him, with his recordings and plans for over-the-top humiliation. It's hard to recover from that in high school. Do we really want people to always remember Asher as the guy who was catfished and had to run around some rich guy's yard naked?"

She shook her head. "And what about Chad?"

"Weirdly, I think Chad's more interested now that I'm sort of taken." This really could be a mutually beneficial arrangement. "He was asking Asher lots of questions about me."

"Uh, if that's not a red flag I don't know what is. I hope that's in your little book of rules: *Any guy who doesn't ask me out for months and only acts interested once I'm taken is off limits.*"

"That's a solid rule." I probably *should* add it.

"But?" Kamala said, knowing there was a *but*.

"But I didn't really give him a chance. I was literally asking him out when Asher came. Maybe he would've said yes." Maybe I'd read his reaction wrong.

"So you're going to date both of them?"

"No, Chad can wait a few more weeks," I said, warming to the idea as I said the words. "He's waited this long."

She made an exploding noise with her mouth as her fingers slowly opened. "Blowing it up."

CHAPTER 7

· · · · · · · · · · · · · ·

Rule: *Never date someone impulsive.*

"Your car is ancient!" Asher yelled from the passenger seat. Bean was sitting on his lap, his head out the window, his tail wagging so hard it was slapping Asher in the arm with every stroke.

When I'd shown up at work that day, Erin had stopped me before I headed to the back and said, "I have a special project for you."

"I was supposed to help Chad with the new intakes today." I tried to peer down the hall to see if I could catch a glimpse of him. I couldn't.

"I'll have Rodrigo help him."

"Oh, okay. What's the project?" I asked.

"It is your solemn duty to find Bean a forever home before the end of summer."

Two months? I had two months? "What? How?"

"You think he'd still be here after two hundred and seventy-nine days if I knew the answer to that question?"

"Read his mind with your twin power," Rodrigo said as he walked by.

"Bean is not my twin," I called after him. "I just sympathize with his hatred of humanity."

Rodrigo laughed loud and long before his laughter was swallowed up by the barking of dogs.

To Erin, I said, "Okay, I'll come up with some sort of plan." Preparation would be important for an assignment like this.

"Today. I want you to work on something today. That's why I called in the volunteer of the month to help you."

"Volunteer of the month? I didn't know we had one of those."

Asher walked in the front doors right at that moment—shirt rumpled, hair windblown, cheeks ruddy—like he had dropped everything and answered a call to save the city. Impulsive. He was impulsive.

"Ah, here he is," Erin said with a clap of her hands. "You two are the only people in the universe that I know of at this moment who that blasted dog likes. It's only fitting you should carry out this mission together."

I raised my eyebrows at her dramatic delivery.

She smiled. "Maybe a field trip?"

I'd taken Bean on several field trips over the months, but since I had no other ideas with so little time to prepare, it was worth a try.

So now Asher and I were in my car, windows down, the rushing wind making it hard to talk. "I know! It's a dinosaur! My dad is very good at his job!" I said.

"You should have his shop's name on the back window as an advertisement. One look at this car and instant business."

I smiled. "Yeah, no, I'm not helping my dad's boss. He's a total tool. I mean, a not very nice guy."

"I know the word *tool*," Asher said. "Why?"

"Why do you know that word? I don't know, maybe because Dale is your friend?"

Asher's eyes shot down and then back up. "No, I meant why is your dad's boss one?"

I internally cursed at myself. *Why did I say that out loud?* Maybe because the wind rushing through the cabin was making it hard to think. "I know that's what you meant. I'm sorry, *I'm* a tool sometimes."

"It's okay, he can be. Especially if you don't really know him."

He was right. I didn't know Dale very well. I had just let my harsh judgment take over. "Where is your sidekick today anyway?"

"His family has been at their cabin this week. He gets home tomorrow."

"Right . . ." Of course Dale had a family cabin.

"Your dad's boss?" Asher asked, reminding me I hadn't answered his original question.

"My dad's boss overworks and underpays him. You know, the age-old plight of the working class."

"Yeah, sounds familiar."

I pulled into the parking lot of the public beach. "Bean loves the water. People won't be able to resist him after I post these pics."

"Over nine months, huh? Is that a long time for a dog to be at the shelter?"

"Yes, very long." I shifted the car into park and turned off the ignition. "And as much as I love ours, shelters aren't great places for dogs. They can be very stressful: noisy, chaotic, cold."

Asher put his hands on either side of Bean's face. "How could a charmer like you go unpicked, Beano?"

I chuckled. "I call him Beano sometimes too." I picked up the scarf that was draped over the parking brake between us and opened my door. "And he's not charming."

Asher climbed out. "Maybe he doesn't want to be picked," he said as we walked across the parking lot and toward the sand. Like most summer days, the beach was packed with people and blankets and umbrellas. We'd have to keep Bean on his leash.

I pulled the baseball cap I wore lower, to shade my eyes from the sun. "You think he wants to stay at the shelter?"

"Maybe he wants to stay with you," he said. "You're easy to be around."

"Am I?" I asked. That wasn't something I heard often. Most of the time I heard I was closed off or cold. Bean's twin, Rodrigo had called me not fifteen minutes ago. Definitely not charming. "*You* are. Maybe *you* should adopt Bean."

"I wish I could but we have this nasty little Chihuahua who would rip him to pieces. It's my mom's dog." We walked a few more steps and then Asher said, "Sorry, no offense, I forgot you like all animals. Buffy has her moments."

I laughed. "I dig the name. And I don't like all animals."

"Really?"

"I genuinely don't like sea lions. They are jerks."

We reached the dark compacted sand, which was wet from the

retreating water. I squatted down and tied the scarf I'd brought around Bean's neck.

"'Adopt me'?" Asher read the big red words printed on the scarf. "That should work."

"People of the beach!" I yelled. "Come adopt this uncharming dog!"

Asher smiled. "He only likes cool people!"

"Or uncool people! We're still trying to decide!"

"I can do this all day," Asher said. "Is this the plan? Yell until someone takes him?"

I lifted my phone. "No, action shots is the plan."

"These are really good," I said, scrolling through the pics Asher had taken. We sat at a table on the pier, sipping cold drinks we'd bought from a food truck. Asher had insisted on buying one of the dog drinks they offered for Bean and he was literally sitting on the ground next to him while holding it. "You look like his butler or something."

"In the pics?"

"No, right now, in real life," I said. "He has you completely under his power."

"How is he not adopted?"

"People are naturally afraid of pits. And his personality doesn't win them over."

As if to prove my point, a woman walked by and paused to smile at him. "Aw, he's up for adoption?"

Bean let out a low growl as she moved to pet him. She immediately stopped in her tracks.

"He is," I said. "And really, he warms up. You interested?"

She pointed over her shoulder. "Um, no, I have a friend who . . ." She started walking before she finished her sentence. I barely heard her mumbled, "Thanks," as she picked up speed.

"You're a tool, Bean," I said. "A total tool."

Asher chuckled, then climbed to his feet and back into the chair next to me, looking over my shoulder as I continued to scroll through pics. Most were action shots, me and Bean running or him fetching a stick, the focus on Bean, me blurry in the background.

"Have you done this before?" Asher asked. "Taken pictures of him outside the shelter?"

"Yes. But these pictures are much better," I added quickly. Although, if I were being honest, they weren't that different. I sighed. "I don't know what else to do for him."

"Maybe something you *haven't* done before?" Asher said.

"Thanks, stellar suggestion."

He laughed. "I'm full of them. How come you didn't want to be in any of the pics?"

I pointed to the blurry me.

"You know what I mean," he said.

I did not like to put myself online. People could say the meanest things behind the privacy of some generic picture and screen name. And although I generally didn't care what a bunch of strangers thought about me, I also didn't feel the need to purposely subject myself to criticism on the regular. "I'm not good at social media. I'm really the last person who should be in charge of social media for the shelter." I turned off my screen and tucked my phone into the front pocket of my backpack.

"Considering how we met and communicated, it's funny to hear you say that you're not good at social media."

His mention of Gemma jolted me out of my pretend bubble. The bubble where hanging out with Asher was perfectly normal. In this bubble we had met in a café and he knew I was me all along and there wasn't this other person lying to him on the side. "I . . . uh . . . that's different."

"How?"

"That's not me putting myself out there for the world to comment on."

"Just one handsome stranger?" He flashed that goofy smile of his. This guy with his floppy hair and lanky arms and silly smirk was pretty adorable.

I shoved his arm with a laugh. "What made you think I wasn't some forty-year-old perv, by the way?"

"Our mutuals and meeting you . . . obviously."

"Obviously." Mutuals? Asher and Gemma had mutual online friends? I wondered who. Did that mean she was actually someone he knew? But if not, had I set Asher up to be kidnapped by some forty-year-old perv by providing *my* face to hide behind? In a panic, I said, "You want my phone number? I mean, do you have it? Have I given it to you? Do you want it? I answer texts faster than DMs."

He looked out at the ocean, a small smile coming onto his face, then he gave a little nod. "Yeah," he said softly. "I want it."

"Okay." We exchanged numbers, then Bean nudged his wet

nose under my hand, asking for scratches. I obliged. "We should get Bean back. Thanks for helping me today."

"It's my job now, my mission," Asher said. "Make people see Bean is lovable by summer's end."

I smiled. "*Our* mission."

He jerked his head toward Bean. "Sit by him and let me take a non-blurry picture." I started to protest, when he said, "It will be something different."

He was right. I did need to try something different.

CHAPTER 8

· · · · · · · · · · · · · ·

Rule: Never date someone who brings out your worst.

"If I got Dad a Brady's Auto Shop sign for his birthday, do you think he'd get the hint and open his own shop already?" I asked my sister. We were at the farmers' market in Old Town, mostly looking and sometimes eating. We'd stopped at a booth that burned words or names or pictures—anything really—into a piece of wood with a laser. We were watching a sign getting made, the words *Will you marry me?* etched into a piece of oak. "He couldn't have splurged on the rustic pine?" I asked.

Zoey looked around. "Shh. Whoever is having that made might hear you." At twenty years old, Zoey was a girl version of our dad: olive skin, dark hair, and kind eyes. And unlike me, she was a people pleaser. She hated disappointing people, even strangers. Even our mom. The second bothered me more than the first.

"Oh no," I teased. "A random person on the street might be mad at me."

She hooked her arm through my elbow and moved us along. "Would your Brady's Auto sign be made of pine?"

"Only the best for Dad," I said.

"It wouldn't work," she said. "Dad will never leave Niles's place."

"I know." Our dad was too set in his ways. Too follow-the-straight-and-narrow.

"Plus, that's a sucky birthday gift." Zoey smiled my way.

I hip-checked her. "I know. What are you getting him?"

The next booth we came to sold handcrafted pens displayed in colorful cases. The smell of kettle corn drifted through the air all buttery sweet.

"I don't know," Zoey said. "Dad's hard to shop for. Maybe we shouldn't have waited until the last minute."

"This was your idea, to get him a gift at the farmers' market! I had the plan to inventory his closet and see what he's missing, remember? We could've been buying him a practical button-down right now. He loves practical."

"You and your plans."

"Plans are good. They work."

"Wren!" a girl called to me from a booth we were passing that boasted jewelry. "Hey!"

"Hi, Stacia!" I yelled back.

"Saw you online!" she called over the crowd. "Way to be a hero!"

"What is she talking about?" Zoey asked.

"Ugh," I groaned. "This is why I never post pics of myself on the shelter's Instagram page."

"You posted one?"

I sidestepped a stroller. "This guy . . . a new volunteer made me. I did it for Bean."

"Bean is still there?"

"Yes! Do you and your roommates need a dog? He's really the best."

"I wish I could, but there's a no-pet policy. Plus, that dog literally sat on my foot and wouldn't move when I met him. But not in a friendly way. In an *I want you to be inconvenienced* way."

I tried not to laugh. She was right, Bean seemed to know exactly what he was doing. He was annoyingly smart like that.

"I don't think he likes me," Zoey said.

"He would like you, eventually, I think." Actually, I didn't think that was true. Bean seemed to form an immediate opinion of someone and never change it. "But maybe tonight at dinner you can help me convince Dad to let me adopt him."

"I will do my best."

We stopped at a booth selling incense—a dozen tall jars lined the table, each holding different scented sticks. I pulled one out and sniffed. Patchouli and rose. "You know who's easy to shop for?" I said.

"Mom," Zoey answered, reading my mind.

"Yep." Our mom collected anything and everything. Pine cones and lotions and hair clips. Whatever she was gifted she loved and obsessed over for a period of time, before moving on to the next thing. "Do you remember the magic beans?"

"Should I?" Zoey asked.

"Wait, you don't?"

"I don't."

"Remember, we were here." I spun a circle with my arms out. "Somewhere on this street during the farmers' market one year and a guy had a booth selling bags of miscellaneous seeds and Mom kept asking him if they were magic beans. He kept telling her no, just seeds from the packing-room floor. But she bought them anyway and insisted they were magic. She planted them in the backyard. I was convinced they would grow into a beanstalk like Jack's."

"And then what happened?" Zoey asked.

"You don't remember this?"

"I don't remember it at all," she said.

"What happened was, she stopped watering them after a while and they shriveled up and died."

Zoey let out a small sigh. "And you took it as some sort of metaphor?"

"I was eight. I didn't know what a metaphor was. But now that you mention it . . ." I shook my head. "*No* memory of this?"

She shrugged. "You seem to remember every little thing Mom did wrong."

And you seem to forget the huge thing. That's what I wanted to say, but I knew Zoey thought I was too harsh on Mom. She always took her side. Another thing I didn't understand about my sister. I gave her a side glance. She was smelling an incense stick. How could she not remember the magic beans? "I'm going to find that guy. I wonder if he still sells his miscellaneous seeds."

"Are you going to buy them this time?" she asked.

"Maybe I will. I'll water them until they grow something."

She raised her eyebrows. "A magic beanstalk?"

"That was Mom's claim, not mine."

She laughed and pulled out her buzzing phone from her pocket. "Speaking of . . . ," she said. On the screen I saw the words *Mom calling.*

"Don't answer that," I said. We were in the middle of a crowded street. Mom could wait.

Zoey didn't listen. She swiped to answer. "Hi, Mom."

My sister had zero boundaries. She really needed a list of her own rules.

She listened for a bit, then said, "Yes, she's with me."

I shook my head and mouthed, *I am not with you.*

"Right here. We're shopping for Dad's birthday. You want to talk to her?" Zoey held the phone out to me.

"Zoe, not cool."

"Just talk to her. It's been a while, right?"

It had been a month, maybe two, since I'd talked to my mom. "If she wants to talk to me she can call me on *my* phone."

"She says she's been trying. Did you block her number again?"

"What?" I asked, feigning innocence. "I would *never.*"

"Wren, just talk to her."

I took her phone, thinking I'd just hang up, but Zoey gave me that pleading look of hers. I sighed. I'd keep it short. "Hello?"

"Wren Bird," my mother sang. "How are you?"

I swallowed, hating that even her voice seemed to stir something in my chest and tighten my throat. "Busy."

"Oh yeah? What's keeping you busy these days?"

"The shelter. I'm trying to home a dog that's been with us long term."

"That sounds like my girl."

I clenched my teeth. What made her think she knew me well enough to know what sounded like me? "What about you?" I said, because after everything she was still my mom and I did wonder.

"I started this rock and crystal business online. I have this tumbler and I find rocks all over. People love shiny things. It lets me explore."

"That sounds like you," I said, because one of us may have changed over the last seven years, but the other one hadn't.

She laughed. I cringed.

"Come visit, Bird."

"Visit what?" I said, completely confused by her statement.

"Me."

"Why?" She'd never asked me that before and it caught me off guard.

"Because it's been too long since I've seen my babies."

"I can't. I work," I said, my voice flat.

"It's summer. You can take some time off."

"No." She'd only visited a handful of times in all these years and now she expected me to drop everything because she decided it was time.

She let out a sharp breath. "Holding on to all this anger can't be good for you."

"Are you seeing a therapist again?" That would be good news. I hoped it might help her sort through her life. The problem was that she would listen to everything her therapist said and apply it to everyone but herself.

"Wren Bird, just think about it, okay?"

"I already thought about it. I don't want to."

"What happened to my free-spirited little girl? Have you lost her?"

I had never been free-spirited. That was always her. And now she wanted a reaction out of me. I wasn't behaving how she wanted, so she was spitting out whatever came into her head. Despite the fact that my eyes felt hot with fire, I was not going to do the same. "I'm hanging up now."

I hung up before she could respond and shoved the phone into my sister's hand. "Don't do that to me again."

"I'm sorry," Zoey said.

Instantly I felt guilty. And I hated that I felt guilty. If I was allowed to be rude to anyone in my life, it was our mom. She left me. She left my sister. She could've left our dad without leaving all of us.

Mom married young, at nineteen, and had Zoey a year later, at twenty. She'd told me once that she married so young to get out of her parents' house, away from the strict rules they felt the need to impose on her even though she was an adult. But with our dad, she still felt stifled. Like she hadn't lived. Maybe he was too regimented for her, too boring. She was determined to have experiences. Every day was riddled with spontaneity. It worked okay when Zoey and I were really little, but once school started, and our mom didn't feel the need to take us or would pull us out midday, she started feeling constrained again. And I started feeling like I had no control over my day. Like I never knew where or when something was going to happen. It was unsettling. I needed rules. I started making rules.

And when she left, I started making more rules, rules about who I could trust. My rules saved me.

And one of those rules was that *I* decided when to see her, not the other way around.

"Are you going to see her?" I asked Zoey, who was staring at the kettle corn truck as if trying to decide if we needed another snack.

"Probably," she said.

"I'm not."

She peeled her eyes away from the popcorn. "I figured."

We walked down the street for several quiet moments. "Gah. Where are the stupid seeds?"

"Maybe he moved on to the next town."

We passed a crate of perfectly ripened tomatoes. "You really don't remember?"

Zoey shook her head.

Maybe my memory was wrong. Maybe there were no magic beans. Maybe a lot of my memories were wrong.

"I'm sorry I made you talk to her," my sister said because she hated it when people were upset with her. "I know it affects you more than me."

"It doesn't affect me at all. I'm fine." Our mom was like a ripple of bad energy. First she soured my mood and now my mood was going to make my sister feel bad. "Let's go find a gift for Dad."

CHAPTER 9

· · · · · · · · · · · · · · · ·

Rule: *Never date a liar.*

Dad, Zoey, and I sat at a small table in Olive Garden, like we did every year for his birthday. Zoey was doing the word search on the back of the kids' menu with a red crayon; Dad was studying his options like he wasn't going to get the same plate of lasagna he ordered every year; and I was checking out the post I'd made of Bean on the shelter's Instagram to see whether anyone had commented.

There were twenty-three likes and only two comments. One just said: *cute.* The other said: *isn't this that mean dog from Adoption Day?*

The shelter held Adoption Day once a month at different places throughout the city. If people didn't want to come to the shelter, we'd waive fees and bring the animals to them. Shopping at the farmers' market? How about taking home a sad dog with that bag of avocados? Giving a pint of blood? Maybe now you have room in your heart for an aging cat! There weren't many local events we didn't try to worm our way into.

I narrowed my eyes at the second comment and deleted it with a jab of my finger. *How's that for mean.*

"Dad," Zoey said, moving a bag stuffed with tissue paper from the bench beside her to the table. "Happy birthday."

"Oh, are we doing that now?" I plopped my gift on the table too.

"Thanks, girls," he said. "You didn't have to."

"Didn't we, though?" Zoey said. "What kind of daughters would we be if we didn't?"

"Broke," I said. "The broke kind. Don't expect too much."

A talkative family walked by our table and was seated at a large one practically an arm's length away. The waitress arrived in front of us with a smile. "You guys ready to order?" She noticed the gifts. "Is it someone's birthday?"

"Yes, it's our dad's," Zoey said.

"You should sing to him later," I added.

"You really shouldn't," Dad said. "Please."

"We won't," she said, then winked at me and Zoey, all but assuring us that she would, in fact, be singing to our dad later.

Dad pointed to a photo on the menu. "I'll have the classic lasagna."

"I want the fettuccine," Zoey said.

"I'll have the eggplant parmigiana," I said when the waitress looked at me.

"Soup or salad?" she asked.

"Salad," Dad answered for us.

"Endless breadsticks," Zoey said.

"Of course," the waitress answered.

The family next to us seemed to have gotten even louder in the last few minutes, laughing and talking over each other as if they shared every thought that came into their heads. The parents sat on one end of the table and I counted, one, two, three . . . my eyes paused. Asher. That was Asher. My eyes shot to the next person and sure enough, it was Brett. Apparently Asher's whole family was here. He had an older sister, it looked like, and an older brother. Then him and Brett.

Asher was speaking at the moment, saying something about school. Something that made him laugh. He laughed with his whole body, his face toward the ceiling, open, like he was.

"Thanks, Zoey," Dad said, bringing my attention back to our table where he was opening my sister's gift. It was a magnetic wristband to hold nuts and bolts and things while working. "This is great."

I shot her a look. She must've gone to the hardware store after the farmers' market. I did not do that. I thought we were both giving him farmers' market finds. Especially considering the farmers' market had been *her* idea.

Our dad moved on to my bag and began taking out the tissue paper. "I heard you blocked your mom's number."

I gasped, then elbowed my sister. "Did you tattle on me?"

"I didn't."

"Your mom told me," Dad said. "Why did you block her?"

Because she would call every day for a week straight and then not call for three months. Sometimes she'd call late at night or in the middle of a school day. She always forgot important dates or holidays. Blocking her allowed me to pretend that she didn't, like

I was not letting her call, not that she was the one who wasn't calling. It gave me the control I needed.

"Because Wren is mean," my sister whispered in a teasing voice. It was a joke I'd heard before, but, in this context, and coming from my people-pleasing sister, it stung.

A basket of breadsticks appeared at our table and I jumped a little, startled. Dad took one, without a response to Zoey's comment, then continued to open my gift. A stupid gift. One I'd gotten at the farmers' market that had nothing my dad would actually like. I should've gone somewhere else, tried harder, stuck to my plan.

"I need to go to the bathroom," I said, standing and darting away from the table. It was obvious why I was fleeing, but neither my dad nor my sister would say a word about it when I got back. That's how the subject of my mom worked—my sister would defend her, my dad would remain neutral, and I came out looking like the irrational one. It was either that or jokes. We were good at joking away anything uncomfortable. It was family tradition.

Instead of going to the bathroom, I went outside. I needed a dose of fresh air to relieve my burning cheeks.

After a couple of minutes of deep-breathing the crisp air, the door behind me pushed open. I turned, expecting to be surprised that my dad or Zoey had actually followed to check on me, but it was just a couple, leaving the restaurant hand in hand.

I turned away and pulled out my phone. I went to Settings, then Blocked Numbers. Hers was the only one on the list. I stared at it for several long minutes and finally clicked on the Unblock button next to her name. I swallowed hard.

"Wren?" There was a tap on my shoulder.

Asher had come outside without making a noise, because there he was, standing next to me. I'd nearly forgotten he was here.

"Hey." I tucked my phone away.

"I thought that was you," he said. "What a coincidence."

"Yeah . . ."

"You must've seen me inside because you don't seem surprised at all."

"Oh, I did. I would've said hi when I . . ." I gestured vaguely to the restaurant.

"Uh-huh, sure you would've," Asher teased, but I could tell his feelings were hurt.

I couldn't handle his feelings right now, I was too busy dealing with my own. "Your family is . . . big."

"They are. And loud."

"I'm sure that's just a result of the sheer number of them."

"That doesn't help." He lowered his brows, a look of concern taking over his face. "You okay?"

No! Not at all. My mother left us when I was only ten and somehow I've become the bad guy in this scenario. For some reason my dad refuses to have an opinion and my sister expects me to play nice. We're supposed to be a united front against her. She chose her life. She can't have it both ways. What would Mr. Big Happy Family think of that speech? "Fine. Just hot" is what I really said.

"Did you see that stupid comment on Bean's post?"

"Yes, I deleted it."

Asher opened his mouth and shut it again. "I didn't know you could do that."

"You didn't know comments could be deleted?"

"I didn't know you held that kind of power," he said.

I laughed, which felt nice. "I'm pretty high up at the shelter."

"Speaking of Bean, I thought of a social media idea that might generate some buzz."

"Generate buzz?" I said with a smile. "You sound like a marketing professional or something."

"Well, it *is* what I want to do."

"You want to be a marketing professional?" I was dying to see his social media now. It was probably so good. Too bad he thought I already knew or I'd ask what his online handle was.

"I know, so aspirational," he said. "What does your son want to be when he grows up? A doctor? A pilot? No, better. He wants to go into marketing."

"Nothing wrong with marketing. It seems everyone needs that these days. And knowing what you want is huge." It was more than I knew about my future at the moment.

"I *do* know what I want," he said in a lowered voice.

My heart seemed to stutter at the comment. I ignored it. "Maybe you should take over the shelter's Instagram."

"I have some ideas, but I'm not going to take that power away from you. I don't have the guts to delete mean comments without a second thought. I'd probably spend my time responding, trying to change their mind, or giving other commenters the chance to refute it."

"How do you know I didn't have a second thought?" I asked.

"Did you?"

I shook my head.

"That's what I thought."

"Because I'm mean," I said.

"What? No. I said the comment was mean, not you."

I waved my hand through the air. "I know. Just a joke."

Asher seemed to sense it hadn't been. "Confident and mean aren't the same thing, Wren."

"You think I'm confident?"

His hazel eyes met mine. "You are."

For all I knew he was talking about Gemma. He hardly knew me, after all. Gemma probably said confident, profound things all the time.

My phone buzzed in my hand. A text from my sister: *Salad's here.*

I jerked my thumb over my shoulder. "I should go eat."

"I should go order," he said.

We walked in side by side over the cream-colored floor tiles with grape accents. Not the color grape. The fruit. A bunch of grapes was painted on every fifth tile. Had someone hand-painted those or were the tiles sold that way?

His family loomed in the distance, all smiles and lively conversation. They looked so animated next to my family. My dad and sister seemed frozen, like a poorly connected FaceTime call.

I suddenly stopped. Asher took two more steps before turning back to look at me with a quizzical expression.

"I'm not your girlfriend," I said. It came out ruder than I meant it to, but my mind had jumped forward to being introduced to his family at the end of this walk. "I mean, for when I meet them. I'm not . . ." Was I making this worse? It wasn't like he'd ever implied

I was. "I'm glad we met and I want to keep getting to know you, but I want to . . ." I wanted to be completely honest, start over, not try to straddle this line of being me and some girl I didn't know.

"Hey," Asher said, leaning forward a bit so his eyes were level with mine. "It's fine. I like how things are too, but we can remain titleless."

I nodded and took a deep breath. "Thank you."

"Asher!" his sister called when we reached the table. "We ordered for you because you were taking too long."

"Cool," he said. "What did I get?"

"It will be a surprise," she said.

"Even better."

Did he mean that? I would not like that kind of surprise.

"Everyone," he said. "This is—"

"Gemma?" his mom asked, eyes going from mildly interested to fully engaged. "Is this her? So nice to meet you!"

"Her name is Wren, Mom," Asher said.

"Wren?" She looked at Asher's dad. "Was that always her name?"

"I thought her name was Elinor," his dad said.

Asher sucked air between his teeth, making the smallest noise, which only I heard. I gave his hand a short squeeze.

"We don't speak that name, Dad!" Brett called out.

"Seriously," his sister said. Speaking of sisters, my eyes darted to my table. Sure enough, *my* sister's attention had turned our way. She had a questioning tilt to her head. My dad was preoccupied dishing salad onto his plate.

"I'm sorry," Asher mumbled. Then, louder, he said, "This is my family. My mom, Cori; my dad, Timothy. That's Leah and Robbie, and you already met Brett," he finished, pointing to his siblings.

"Hi, everyone," I said.

"We heard you were a world-class dungeon master," Cori said.

"What now?" I asked.

"We heard you were joining the D&D campaign tomorrow with Asher's friends. Did I get that wrong too?" she asked, eyes wide and on Asher now.

"No, Mom. She is."

"World class?" Brett asked. "Is there a worldwide ranking system for D&D?"

All eyes were on me now, waiting for a response. I had no clue what they were even talking about. "I, um . . ."

"Guys, leave her be or she won't want to come tomorrow," Asher said.

"Who knew you'd find a girl who liked D&D as much as you do," his sister said.

My sister's face was contorted with confusion. She was probably just as lost as I was. "Yep, D&D forever," I said.

Asher chuckled beside me.

"Please join us," Cori said, moving toward another table, ready to pull an empty chair over.

"That's okay," I said quickly. "I'm with my family." I shouldn't have gestured when I said it because suddenly the whole table was calling out hellos to my dad and sister. Unlike Asher's family, who had *heard so much about me*—well, Gemma—I hadn't said a word about Asher to anyone except Kamala.

"I'm sorry," Asher said, seeming to recognize my overwhelmed expression even without having seen it before.

"We should join our tables together," Cori said.

"Mom," Asher said in a loud but friendly voice, "no. We're not going to do that. We are going to let them eat in peace."

I gave them the stiffest smile and slinked away to my table.

"What was *that* about?" Zoey asked, raising her eyebrows.

"He's a volunteer at the shelter," I said, because that was really the only true thing I could say.

"Thanks for my gift, Bird," Dad said, holding up a leather-bound journal stamped with his initials. Why had I gotten him that? My dad wasn't one to sit around writing down his innermost thoughts.

"You don't have to use it," I said.

"I will," he assured me.

"No, but really," Zoey persisted. "Who *are* those people? Since when do you play Dungeons and Dragons?"

That's what D&D stood for? I was screwed. "Since tomorrow, I guess."

A small group of waiters came with our food and a slice of chocolate cake with a lit candle on top. They sang "Happy Birthday"—badly—to our dad, who looked like he wanted to melt into the floor. Asher's family joined in, saving the song but causing our dad's cheeks to redden even more.

"Are they for real?" my sister asked, eyes scanning Asher's table.

"Very real."

CHAPTER 10

· · · · · · · · · · · · · ·

Rule: *Never date someone you can't
be yourself around.*

"You told him I was coming too, right?" Kamala asked the next
day from behind the wheel of her car. We were on our way to Asher's house and my stomach felt like it was in a million tiny knots.

"No, I didn't. I'm not sure how this game works and I didn't
want to give him the chance to say no."

"Thanks," she said sarcastically.

"My nerves are overruling any other feelings right now, so your
guilt trip is not working."

"It will be fine. Read me some of the rules you found online
again." She nodded toward my phone, which was in my lap

"There are no clear rules! It's like an improv game. And there
are a number of different dice that might be used, none of which I
understand, but apparently they all have a million sides to them."

"I'm not going to say you got yourself into this and I don't feel
sorry for you, but . . ." Zoey trailed off with a hum.

"And now you're in it with me."

"True," she said. "I hate you."

I put my face in my hands and groaned.

"Maybe tonight you come clean?"

"Yeah, maybe." I knew I should. I couldn't even remember why I was doing this. To save a guy I hardly knew from humiliation? To help him restore his confidence after a bad breakup? To make Chad jealous? Those didn't seem like good enough reasons anymore.

"Asher seems to have some sort of magical powers of persuasion over you," Kamala said.

"He does not," I insisted, but if I were being honest with myself, he did. He had charisma, an openness and optimism that were like pure sunlight drawing people in. It was an addictive feeling, but one I didn't trust at all. It's how my mom made people feel . . . until she didn't.

"Is this it?" Zoey asked as we pulled up in front of the house with the bright blue door.

"Yes."

"Let's go."

I picked up the plastic container of cookies I had bought earlier today and got out of the car.

The walkway was lit, as was the porch, and Kamala rang the doorbell the second we stepped onto it.

"What?" she asked when I gasped. "Did you want to wait here and be anxious for several minutes?"

"Yes, I did."

She laughed and the door swung open to reveal Asher and Dale, our official welcoming committee. Asher had not told me that Dale would be here too. He didn't seem like the D&D type.

"Hi. This is Kamala." I thrust the container of cookies forward.

"You named the cookies?" Asher asked, taking them and ushering us inside. "Individually? Or is that what they're known as collectively?"

"Funny," I said. We walked into a small front room that housed a pair of couches that looked like they'd never been sat on. They were a pale cream, with carved wood trim along the back and arms. Show couches. I wondered if we would've had show couches if Mom still lived with us. When she moved out, we had moved shortly after, into a smaller house. "No, the cookies are for you or your friends or whoever. This is my friend Kamala." I presented Kamala like she was a guest on a talk show, holding out both my hands in her direction.

"You're Coffee Shop Girl," Dale said.

"Yes, I work at the coffee shop," Kamala said

"I tried working once," Dale said. "At Wren's shelter. I decided it wasn't for me."

I rolled my eyes.

"He's kidding," Asher said to me. "I told him to try not to act like a rich snob around you and apparently he's decided to lean into it."

"When we were stalking you online," Kamala said, "we saw you were loaded."

Dale gave her a half smile. "I'm disappointed in myself for not being better prepared for online stalkers. I don't have nearly enough shirtless pics on my page right now."

"There were plenty," Kamala said with a laugh.

"Did you like the short shorts one?"

"I mean, I didn't click the little heart or anything. What kind of stalker would that make me?"

"But you liked it?"

Kamala giggled. Like actually giggled. Maybe I should've left her at home.

"So wait, you work at the coffee shop where Asher met you for the first time." Dale pointed first to Kamala and then to me.

Oh, right, this was the main reason I was keeping up the charade—Dale's suspicions. In all my stressing over D&D rules I hadn't thought about the Kamala connection to our first meeting.

"I suggested the coffee shop," I said. "Can't be too safe when meeting strangers."

Asher paused as though about to correct me, as though about to tell me that *he* actually suggested the meeting place. But I was saved by a little Chihuahua that came tearing down the hall, yipping loudly as it did. It ended up at my feet, where it began to run circles around me.

"You must be Buffy," I said over the noise.

"Sorry," Asher said, scooping her up. She immediately quieted but stared at me with bulging eyes.

"It's okay, Slayer," I said. "We'll be friends soon." I wasn't trying to be cocky, but I hadn't met a dog I couldn't win over. People were a different story.

"You don't want that dog to like you," Dale said. "It has a leg-humping problem."

"I do have pretty irresistible legs."

"No comment," Dale said.

We paused for a few moments longer in the room with the nice couches, like we were all waiting for something to happen.

"Come on," Asher said, holding Buffy in one arm and pointing the container of cookies toward the hall in front of us like it wasn't the one and only option.

As we walked, noise—talking and laughter—filtered down the hall and my nerves flared again. We rounded the corner to a great room attached to the kitchen. Asher's mom was at the island putting out food and chatting to the two people in the great room standing by the couch. I had expected a larger group.

His mom spotted me and said, "Welcome, welcome, Wren!" Then her eyes found Buffy, still in Asher's arm. "Oh no, is she bugging you? She can be such a handful, but she's sweet. I'm sure you've had to deal with lots of dogs that are much worse. Right?" she asked me like she needed reassurance that she didn't own Satan's dog.

"Much worse," I said, because that was actually true. "Buffy is nothing. I mean, she's very normal . . . doglike."

"Wren brought cookies," Asher said, saving me from whatever hole I seemed to be falling down.

Asher deposited Buffy outside the back door, then set the cookies on the counter. His mom oohed and aahed over them like they weren't just a dozen store-bought cookies.

"They're probably too crispy," I said, because apparently I didn't do well with praise.

"I love crispy," Cori said. She rounded the island and came over to me. "I'm so glad you made it." She squeezed my shoulders and brought me in for a short hug. "And who's this?" She turned to Kamala and hugged her as well.

"This is my friend Kami," I said.

"Welcome, both of you. Eat and have fun and try not to die. May your rolls bring you luck tonight." With that she left.

Kamala blinked. "She's so mommy."

"The mommiest," I said.

I hadn't meant for Asher to hear me, but he obviously had. "Sorry," he said. "My mom is easily excitable."

"She's nice," I assured him.

"Aggressively nice."

I gave a laugh. "Is that where you get it from?"

"You think I'm aggressively nice?"

"Like the little puppies we get in at the shelter, climbing all over each other to give their love to the closest recipient."

"Good thing puppies are your favorite." He smirked as he walked toward the others.

A smile spread across my face.

"No wonder he can persuade you to do anything," Kamala said. "That nerd is charming."

I nodded. "Too charming." Sunlight.

"Guys," Asher said. "This is my . . . um . . . Wren and her friend Kamala. They are experts at the game, so no need to take it easy on them."

"Actually," I said. "Kamala is a D&D virgin. She needs lots of hand-holding."

"Thanks," Kamala mumbled, "for that visual."

"I volunteer," Dale said. "For the hand-holding." As if I had meant it literally, he came and collected Kamala by the hand and took her to the far side of the room, where he offered her a seat on an oversized armchair, barely big enough for the two of them. I watched her for a few minutes to make sure she didn't need me to save her, but she was laughing and flirting right along with him. The little traitor. So much for my plan to use her game ignorance to help me learn. She was getting a personal lesson.

"I turn the floor over to Darren," Asher said. "The dungeon master."

A guy in a Pokémon T-shirt stepped to the head of the coffee table. Behind him was a brick fireplace and he looked so somber standing there. He took out a fancy notebook and turned back the cover. Each person held a little velvet sack full of dice. Were they going to share them? I definitely didn't bring a sack of dice.

"How long has this campaign been going on?" I asked when Asher joined me, proud of myself for remembering that word from the internet.

"It's a home brew. We actually just started this one last week for the summer, so you haven't missed much."

I had no idea what *home brew* meant, but I nodded like I did.

The other guy sat down on the couch. Asher gestured to the love seat and he and I sat side by side.

"When last we met," Darren said in a deep affected voice, "we were forced to leave the walled city due to the explosion of Clint's spell and the townspeople ousting us."

"Sorry," Clint said.

"We now convene at a fork in the road. To the right, fog hangs low over the swampy path." Darren crouched and held out his hand like he was trying to sweep the fog away. "To the left is a dry barren wasteland." Now he held his hand up to the sky as though blocking the sun.

"Aren't we forgetting something?" Clint said. "Wren and Kamala haven't introduced their characters."

Darren sighed, as though irritated. He shot Asher a look but then bowed and gestured toward me.

I froze. "Kamala can go first," I finally spit out.

"She's just going to be my partner today," Dale said. "An observer."

Everyone seemed to accept that, no problem.

"Me too," I said. "I'll be Asher's partner."

"No way," Asher said, a twinkle in his eye. "I know you want to play."

"What are you?" I asked. "Your character, I mean."

"A dragonborn paladin."

For a split second my mouth fell open. I quickly shut it.

"Pretty cool, right?" he said.

"Yeah." I'd let him think that's why I looked shocked, but in reality, it was because I had no idea what any of that meant.

"Did you bring your character sheet?" Asher asked.

"Oh, um . . . I forgot it."

"You forgot?" Darren asked. "Were you expecting us to wait while you built your character here?"

Asher smiled toward Darren. "It's fine. I have a couple backup characters." He got up and ran out of the room.

I sat there with my hands folded in my lap and gave Kamala a wide-eyed look, wondering if it was too late to run out of the house. I had thought I could wing it, figure this game out in context, but I was totally wrong. She covered her mouth as though stifling a laugh.

Clint raised his hand a little. "I'm a tiefling artificer."

What was happening? Was that English or did he just start speaking a made-up D&D language? "Cool," I squeaked out.

"Don't get him started on his Tinkertoys," Dale said.

"Definitely won't do that," I said.

Asher came back, breathless and holding several pieces of paper. "Who do you want to be? A gnome wizard or a half-elf bard?" As he held up the papers, I saw staples in the top corners, which meant there was more than one page of explanations. I was in way over my head. "The elf," I said. At least I'd heard of that before.

"Going with the chaotic-evil alignment. Interesting," Asher said with a smirk, handing me the papers reverently, along with my own velvet bag of dice.

I scanned the first page. At the top was a shield with the number fourteen on it. The rest of the page was a series of boxes, each of which contained words like *strength, dexterity, constitution, intelligence,* and *health* and with a corresponding number.

The game proceeded after my pick. I knew that wasn't the extent of my participation. I was going to have to do something, not just exist. I was screwed.

My phone buzzed in my pocket. I hoped it was Kamala giving me an excuse to flee. But it wasn't. It was my mom. I'd forgotten I unblocked her, and seeing her name on the screen made my tense body that much tenser.

"Did you get bad news?" Asher whispered as Clint talked about wanting to investigate the wooden sign at the fork in the road. "You look like you got bad news."

"No." I turned my phone to face him when I realized *I* hadn't even read the text. My eyes quickly scanned it. *Your sister is coming and I hope you will too, Bird.*

It didn't surprise me that Zoey had decided to visit Mom. She liked to pretend her leaving seven years ago was a normal part of every mom's journey. I didn't like to pretend. I clenched my jaw thinking about what I was doing this very moment. *Never date someone you have to pretend for, Wren.*

"Bird?" Asher asked, his hand brushing my arm.

A shiver went down my back. "Wren. It's a bird."

"Oh yeah, it is. That's cute."

It had always been my dad's nickname for me. I hated it when my mother started using it.

"Or not," he said, reading my expression. "She should use your real name or nothing at all."

I smiled. Even though I knew he was joking, it was nice to have someone back me up.

Clint rolled one of his dice—a sparkling gold one with lots of sides. Everyone groaned.

The dungeon master said, "The wooden sign was just a wooden sign. It gave no hints on what lay ahead."

This led to an in-depth discussion on who thought they were better suited for what environment. Clint affected an odd accent that he hadn't used until that moment. Asher used his own voice, and I wondered if he was doing that for me. If he normally gave his dragonborn thingy a deep dragon voice, like in *Lord of the Rings*.

"I think I'm a swamp girl," I said, pretending to study my paper.

Asher gave me a sideways glance. "You think so, huh?"

"Swamps are cool," Kamala said.

Darren and his serious eyes stared her down.

Asher laughed. "To the swamp!"

CHAPTER 11

· · · · · · · · · · · · · · · · ·

Rule: *Never date someone too nice. You might
blow them up.*

Apparently, I wasn't a swamp girl or I sucked at rolling dice or I
knew nothing about the game I was playing or the strengths of my
character because I died. The ghost of a goblin murdered me and
my death-save rolls were worthless. The crushing disappointment
I felt at my death surprised me. I wanted to do better at the game.
To be a natural, or something.

Perhaps reading my expression, Asher turned to the dungeon
master and said, "She can rejoin as another character, right?"

"No!" Clint boomed, and continued in his affected voice. "Her
death is true and final. There is no reincarnation in this world."

Kamala let out a little giggle.

Asher tilted his head and was about to say something else when
I reached for his arm. "It's fine. I should stay dead."

My phone had been buzzing for the last hour, and my head
had been buzzing at least half that long from trying to pretend I

actually knew what I was doing. "I need to respond to some texts anyway. I'll be right back."

Asher nodded, and I left the great room and pulled out my phone to see a string of texts from my mom. I read through them as I walked slowly down the hall, which was lined with family pictures. Not just the ones where the subjects had stiff smiles and were posed in awkward formations (although there were some of those as well) but also candid shots taken at parks and by lakes and at weddings. I couldn't remember the last time my family had *printed* a picture, let alone framed it and hung it on a wall.

Zoey is coming for the Fourth of July. It will be beautiful up here. They do fireworks over the lake.

There's so much to do up here and it's gorgeous.

We could hike and camp.

My mom lived in Northern California, near Lake Tahoe. At least that's where she lived the last time I asked. She liked to move a lot, but Zoey hadn't mentioned her moving. And what she was describing sounded like that area. I'd never been.

You're my daughter, Wren, and I miss you.

Please think about it.

Her tone was different from the past. Maybe she really was seeing a therapist and learning how to speak to people—like they had a choice in the matter.

I had walked the entire length of the hall, taking in a lifetime of pictures, and arrived at the end, where a bedroom door stood open. I held on to the doorframe as I took in the room. A twin bed with a dark comforter was on one side; on the other was a large desk with an elaborate computer setup. Pinned to the wall around the computer were posters that I couldn't read, but I could tell were old.

I leaned against the doorframe and typed, *I'll think about it.*

I immediately felt terrible. I erased the sentence. Was there a sentence even less committal than *I'll think about it?*

"*No* is a full sentence, Wren," I mumbled. I didn't type anything. I didn't have to tell her I'd think about it to think about it. My sister would be there. We'd have fun. I hadn't been to Lake Tahoe.

Buffy the dog peered around the corner.

"Hello," I said, lowering myself to the floor. "You're not going to bark at me this time?" I leaned against the wall and stretched my legs out in front of me. I put one hand, palm up, on the ground and Buffy inched forward warily. She reached out her nose and sniffed my hand. "Such a good girl," I said in a soft voice. She peered up at me. "Any advice on dealing with moms?"

She practically tiptoed into my lap and curled up.

"I'm not willing to try this with my mom." I gently ran my hand down her head and back.

Asher poked his head into the hall. "Hey, did you get lost?" He smiled big. "Oh, I see, you've found your real friend."

"I mean, she didn't let me get killed in a game, so . . ."

He watched Buffy for a moment. "I'm impressed."

"I'm practically Snow White. I just need to find some hidden forest free of people where I can live out my days."

"Wasn't Snow White surrounded by men?" Asher said with a flirty half smile.

"True. Her first mistake." I pointed at the open bedroom door. "Is this your room?"

"It is."

"What's up with the posters?"

He walked the length of the hall and held out his hand to help me up. I tucked Buffy under one arm and reached out my other hand for him. He pulled me to standing. My shoulder bumped his chest.

"Sorry," he said.

"Why?" I asked.

He put his hand on my lower back, steadying me. I met his eyes, which were crinkled at the corners with his smile. My breath caught.

"You want to see the posters?" he asked.

"What?"

"In my room?"

"Oh, right." I placed Buffy on the floor and followed Asher in as he flipped on the light.

I walked to his desk to get a closer look. One of the posters was of three old ladies, one of whom was screaming into a corded phone. Big yellow words above their heads read: *Where's the beef?* Another poster had a woman with a milk mustache and the words *Got milk?* next to her.

"What in the . . . ?" I asked, finally turning around.

"Remember all the old memes I used to DM you?"

I coughed a little. My body apparently hated telling lies. "Yeah, of course."

"I like to study patterns in media and why popular advertising worked in its respective era." Asher shrugged. "I told you I'm a marketing nerd."

"Wow," I said. "I had no idea how deep you'd fallen into the marketing hole."

"Tell me you've heard of these ad campaigns. I mean . . ." He pointed to the Nike swoosh with the words *Just Do It* beneath it. "This started in 1988! And it's still going strong. Why? Because it's catchy, it's memorable."

I nodded slowly.

"Speaking of: the Bean Games!"

"What?"

"Last night at Olive Garden I was trying to tell you that I thought up a campaign for Bean that might generate some buzz."

"Oh, right," I said. "This buzz we need generated. What are the Bean Games?"

"We recruit people to participate in different events. Their competitor? Bean."

"Like what? Fetch?"

"Sure, or a puppuccino drinking contest. Who can drink it the fastest?"

"You're going to make humans drink one of those dog coffees?" I asked.

"They're mostly just whipped cream, right? It would be funny. And it would . . ."

I smiled. "Generate buzz?"

"Exactly! We'll do one competition a week and have sign-ups on Instagram to be a future participant."

My mind spun as I thought about the idea. It was something

we hadn't tried before. It would get people interacting with Bean. And if he wasn't a jerk, it could work. "Hey, you should go into marketing when you grow up."

"My parents would be so proud."

"I have a feeling your parents would be proud no matter what you did. They seem aggressively proud."

"They are. They really are."

How would that be? I wondered. I probably wouldn't like it. If my dad was proud about everything, wouldn't that basically mean all accomplishments were equal? But I could do with a little *occasionally proud*. That would require a parent who didn't work so much, or who wasn't constantly trying to play Switzerland in every serious conversation. Or maybe it would require me being more open. I wasn't sure any of those things were possible.

As if reading my mind, Asher asked, "What about your dad?"

"Sorry I didn't introduce you at the restaurant."

"It's okay, you were busy running from my family."

I smiled. "This is true."

"Proud dad? Or surly dad?"

Were those the only two options? Did they represent either end of the parent spectrum? I wanted to just say, *Yes, my dad is super proud,* but I found myself saying, "I don't share much with my dad. He has too much to worry about."

"Are accomplishments something to worry about?"

"There aren't many of those to share."

"I find that hard to believe," Asher said.

"Well, I'm no marketing professional."

"Ha!"

My cheeks went pink. It wasn't like he was hard to make laugh—the opposite, in fact—but his laugh was so genuine and open. "I like your idea for Bean. Thanks for taking this seriously," I said.

"Every ounce of seriousness I have is directed toward this project."

"You're being aggressively serious?"

His smile fell off his face. "Yes, I am."

"Oh!" I said, suddenly remembering we weren't in the house alone. "The game. Are they all waiting for us?"

"No, I died. Darren had it out for us tonight."

"I sensed that. Was he mad I came or something?"

Asher cringed. "Not mad, exactly. Just mad I didn't tell him a week in advance. He puts a lot of work into these. Sorry he went hard on you."

I wouldn't have known the difference either way. "My rolls were off, too," I said.

"Yeah, they were," he agreed.

Dale's head appeared in the bedroom doorway, followed by his whole body. "I see how it is, you guys ditch us with the nerds."

Kamala was right behind him. "That's a fun game. I like your friends."

"But you like me the best, right?" Dale said.

"Of course." Like I had, she walked over to the posters on the wall. " 'Where's the beef?' "

"He's a marketing genius," I whispered.

"Did you design these?" Kami asked.

"I wish!" Asher said without a hint of sarcasm.

I couldn't help but laugh. I summarized Asher's idea about the Bean Games to Kamala and Dale.

"I like it," Kamala said. Then she raised her eyebrows at me and I couldn't quite read what she was trying to say, but I sensed it was something like, *See, he's really nice, your lies are going to blow him up.* Or maybe she wasn't saying that at all and I was just projecting.

"All this to home a dog?" Dale asked. "Why doesn't anyone want him? What's wrong with him?"

"Nothing is wrong with him," I said. "It's people who have all the issues."

I wasn't sure what kind of look Asher was giving Dale behind my back, but the next words out of his mouth surprised me. "Well, we can have the first Bean Game at my house."

CHAPTER 12

• • • • • • • • • • • • • • •

Rule: *Never let the guy you want to date hang out*
with the guy you're sort of dating.

"What are you doing?" a voice from behind me asked.

I jumped up from attaching a leash to Bean's collar and turned around. "Chad, you scared me."

Bean let out a single bark.

"Don't worry. I'm not stealing your girl," Chad said to Bean.

I laughed. Chad *did* know how to tell a joke. But his face was serious, with no hint of it being a joke at all. I turned my laugh into throat clearing.

"Sorry, I didn't mean to scare you," Chad said. "Are you taking Bean somewhere?" He stood on the other side of the chain-link door, staring into Bean's kennel. He was still as cute as ever with that dark hair and cut jaw. He was also holding a leash, the sweet corgi from the other day on the other end.

"Where are you taking her?"

"Francesca has been adopted."

"Really? Is she staying with her brothers?"

"Yes, all three have been homed together."

"That's amazing." I never thought the three would get to stay together. Hopefully there was some of that elusive magic left over for Bean. "Me and some friends are going to have a puppuccino drinking contest for an online game we're starting to try to home Bean. When people see the video, hopefully they'll sign up for the next contest."

"Oh, right. The impossible task: Place him before the end of summer."

I covered Bean's ears and gasped. "Watch your mouth."

Chad calmly looked at Bean standing there. Chad was always relaxed and steady, like he was grounded in reality—things I'd always appreciated about him. Bean did not return his gaze.

I patted Bean's neck. "You don't think it's possible?"

"*You* do? That dog has been here forever."

"We just need a miracle," I said.

"I don't believe in those," Chad said.

I usually didn't either, but Asher and his *generating buzz* talk had turned me into a believer. "Yeah, well, a little hope never hurt anyone." I made sure Bean's leash was secure and stood. His tail immediately started wagging with the knowledge that we were leaving his kennel.

Chad, still on the other side of the door, said, "Can I help? I just need to pass Francesca off to Rodrigo and then I'm done for the day."

"If you don't mind drinking a dog coffee," I said, "you're in."

Chad had insisted we use one of the dog seat belts from the shelter, and much to Bean's frustration, he was in the back seat of my car, unable to move very far. It was probably safer for all of us this way, but I felt like Bean spent most of his life trapped, so I liked to let him stick his head out the window.

"I know," I said. "Chad is a meanie."

Chad let a breath out his nose. "I'm the only one who cares about your life, Bean. Maybe you should love *me* instead." He reached his hand back and I watched in the rearview mirror as Bean turned his head, pressing it against the seat, in a rebuff.

"Ouch," I said. "Rejected."

"Whose house are we going to again?" Chad asked.

"Dale's. He's Asher's friend."

"Dale . . . the guy who worked check-in last time?"

"Yeah."

"He wants to be a social media influencer or something," Chad said.

I didn't realize Chad had talked to him at all. I thought he'd only been asking Asher the questions. "Was he recording? He does that a lot."

"He wants to go viral," Chad said.

"Doesn't everybody?"

"I don't," Chad said.

"Yeah, me neither."

"And Asher. You're still seeing him?"

"We're hanging out," I said. I didn't want to completely deter the guy who I'd always thought was right for me for the one who was completely wrong. Because really that was all Asher and I were doing—hanging out. We hadn't gone on a date. We hadn't kissed. He hadn't even hugged me since I declared to him I wasn't his girlfriend at Olive Garden. My mission hadn't changed: I was helping him save face. And *eventually* telling him the truth once I knew Dale wasn't going to follow through with his humiliation plan. Kamala said he'd asked a lot of questions about me at D&D night. She'd tried to keep it vague but sensed he was digging.

"What have you been doing this summer?" I asked, changing the subject.

"Not much. Working. I'm going up to Lake Tahoe for the Fourth, so that should be fun."

My head whipped in Chad's direction, but I quickly glued my eyes back to the road. A light ahead turned red and I lifted my foot off the gas.

"What?" he asked.

"Nothing. It's just my mom wants me to visit for the Fourth. She lives near there."

"You should. That would be fun."

"No, I . . . yeah, maybe," I said. "I still haven't decided."

"The Fourth is not that far away."

"I know. I need to decide."

"Why wouldn't you go?"

This was where I should've told him about my nonexistent relationship with my mom, but that was so much baggage to dump on someone. Especially on someone I *eventually* wanted to date. "I hate to leave my dad alone on holidays." That was true too.

The directions on my phone guided us into a neighborhood in the hills.

"Well, if you do end up going, let me know. My aunt lives there and my cousins always take me to some fun parties on the Fourth. I'm sure they wouldn't care if you came too."

"I'll probably be hanging out with my mom and sister, but yeah, if I have some time that day, I'll text you." I pulled up in front of a huge Spanish-style house. There was a large paved circular drive and a meticulously manicured hedge leading up to imposing wood double doors.

"This is where he lives?" Chad asked.

"I know, right?" I said.

Another car had pulled up at the same time and it took me a second to realize it was Kamala. She pointed to the driveway and then shrugged, asking if we were allowed to drive on it. I shrugged right back.

"Is that Kamala?" Chad asked.

"Yes, she's bringing the doggie coffee. I'm bringing the dog."

"Are you going to pull in?"

"My car feels too junky for that driveway. I should park on the street." One time I parked in our driveway at home and my car decided to leak oil all over. Dad poured cat litter on it and kept it like that for several days. This wasn't a cat-litter-driveway kind of neighborhood. I pulled up to the curb and turned off my car.

Kamala turned into the driveway and parked next to Asher's Toyota, which was already near the side gate.

"This neighborhood is insane," Kamala said when I met up with her, Bean and Chad in tow. She was holding a drink carrier full of puppuccinos.

"I know."

"Hey, Chad," she said. "I didn't know you were coming."

That was for me. It was a reprimand. This was probably her validation that I was going to blow everything up.

She was probably right. Why had I let him come? Chad being here with me would just be more evidence for Dale's suspicions.

"Hello, Bean," Kamala said.

He scratched at one of the paving stones as if to show her that he wasn't interested.

"Maybe you'd be nicer to me if you saw me slaving over your dog drinks."

"He wouldn't," Chad assured her.

"Is one of them dairy-free?" I asked. The white foam topping filled up at least three-quarters of each cup. Kamala liked to brag that they did their doggie coffees different from most places. It wasn't just the whipped cream—there was a dog-safe drink below that as well.

"Yes, the one that says *Baby* on the side is for you."

I laughed. "If I could control my stomach do you think I would tell it to deprive me of ice cream?"

"Your stomach, the only thing you can't control." Kamala gave me her teasing smile.

I wish that was the only thing I couldn't control. My whole life was feeling pretty out of control at the moment.

We let ourselves through the gate and into Dale's backyard. It was even more impressive than the front. Large squares of stamped concrete, each one bordered with tightly trimmed grass, surrounded a massive pool, complete with a pool house. Near the pool was a firepit surrounded by stone benches. And on the far side of the yard was an expansive grass area lined with trees and flowers.

That's where Asher was, along with Dale and Brett. They were setting up a short table made out of a piece of plywood balanced on top of four cinder blocks. It looked out of place in the fancy yard. Asher looked up as we arrived and smiled at me. My stomach gave a surprising jolt and I pressed my palms against it.

Next to me, Kamala raised her eyebrows.

"No comment," I responded.

"I want to see if this dog likes me," Brett announced, and he walked our way and sat on the ground at least twenty feet from Bean. "Come here, boy."

Bean stared, uninterested, then turned a one-eighty, presenting him with his backside.

"Wow," Brett said, hopping up and walking over. "He didn't have to make it so obvious."

"Are you going to drink a dog drink today?" I asked him.

"I'm always up for fun in the name of social media views. Right, Dale?"

Dale, phone already out, joined us in time to hear Brett's statement. "Everything is about social media views."

"Well, this is actually for a cause, but sure," I said.

"Which will only be spread through social media views."

I couldn't argue with him there. "True."

Asher came strutting over and immediately greeted Bean by dropping to the ground next to him. "Hey, Good Boy," he said, scratching behind his ears. Bean's tongue lolled out of his mouth and his tail went crazy. He placed his paws on Asher's knees and licked his face several times. "Are you ready to beat these suckers in a coffee-drinking contest?"

Bean gave him a single bark.

"Well, aren't you the dog whisperer," Dale said, recording the exchange.

"Seriously," Kamala said.

Asher climbed to his feet. "Hey," he said to me. I thought he'd lean in for a hug. I even prepared myself for it, opening my arms a bit, but he didn't. He turned to Chad. "You brought a recruit."

"I did." I dropped my arms and pretended to mess with Bean's leash.

"Hopefully this video will make it so potential adopters will sign up for the next one," Asher said.

"I hope," I said.

"I don't know," Chad said. "People might be wary about something like this."

"They might," Asher said in his good-natured way. "But *not* trying definitely won't work."

An awkward silence fell over the group.

"Where should I put these?" Kamala asked, lifting the coffee carrier.

"Follow me," Asher said.

Dale sniffed the dog coffee. "Is this going to be nasty?" he asked.

He was on his knees along with Asher, Brett, Chad, and me.

Kamala held her camera phone, ready to film. Bean was next to me, sitting like the goodest boy. I had my hand over his coffee and mine. The plan was to let go after Kamala's countdown and hope Bean looked fun and playful on camera. Which, for the right people, he was.

"It's not bad," Kamala said. "I've tasted it before."

"Really? Why?" Dale asked.

"So that when people ask if it's safe I can say, yes, it is. It's made with all-natural ingredients. *I've* even tried it."

"Do you say it just like that?" Brett asked.

"Pretty much."

Asher looked down the line. His cup was on the table in front of him. "Is everyone ready?"

"Are we picking it up and drinking it?" Chad asked. "Or literally drinking it like a dog?" He was at the very end of the line, farthest away from me. I wondered if Asher had done that on purpose. That thought made a chuckle work its way up the back of my throat. I quickly squelched it.

"However you want to do it," Asher said, "but you can't use your hands."

"Gross," Chad muttered.

"Is everyone ready?" Kamala asked, her finger hovering over the Record button. She glanced my way.

"Are you ready, Bean?" I asked. He obviously had no idea what was going on, but he gave me a happy bark anyway.

"Three . . . two . . ."

I uncovered the cup and patted the table. Bean moved forward.

"One!"

"Up, Bean," I said, hoping he'd put his paws on the table and dig in. "Treat."

Bean lunged forward and stuck his nose in the cup. To my right, Asher had his tongue in the cup. I laughed and picked up my cup with my teeth, tilting it back and trying to dump its contents in my mouth. I got a faceful of liquid. "Ugh." The cream wasn't budging. I put the cup back on the table and sucked in a big mouthful followed by another. That's when Bean licked the side of my face.

"This is disgusting," Brett said. "What is it again?"

Bean tipped over his cup and as the contents spilled across the table my eyes caught the word *Baby* on the side in Kamala's handwriting. "Oh crap." Bean jumped on top of the table as I tried to spit anything left in my mouth onto the grass. That's when Bean noticed the line of people with their treats. I grabbed for his leash but missed as he barreled across the table, knocking over cups as he went.

When he got to the end, where Chad was kneeling, he sneezed in his face and jumped down.

Dale was on his feet, brushing off his jeans with his hands. "These are my nice jeans."

"Why'd you wear nice jeans to a dog competition?" Brett wondered aloud.

Chad was making disgusted noises, wiping up doggie snot and doggie drink with the bottom of his shirt.

Bean kept running. "Halt! Sit! Stay!" I yelled one command after the next as I chased after him, wiping my face on the sleeve of my shirt. I finally got him under control before he could bolt out the side gate with me in tow. He sat, acting like he had been listening the entire time. His expression as he looked up at me seemed to ask, *Why are you out of breath?*

"You know why," I mumbled to him.

I turned to see Asher come skidding to a halt.

"I thought you might need some muscle," he said, then looked at Bean. "But he . . . he's fine."

I smirked. "Were you going to be the muscle?"

"I've been told I'm very strong."

"By your aggressively nice mom?"

He laughed, then pushed his floppy hair off his forehead. "Well, that was a disaster."

"You think we have anything usable?"

He nodded enthusiastically. "It will be funny. I'll edit something together and shoot it over to you later."

"What? No, I'll edit it." This was my actual job. He was a volunteer. I wasn't going to make him do anything more than he'd already done.

"It's easy for me," he said. "I have all the software and stuff."

"It's fine. I got it."

"Miss I'm Bad at Social Media has it?"

"I do," I said. I hated counting on someone else to do something for me, wondering whether they were going to follow through. Doing it myself saved us all disappointment.

Asher held up his hands in surrender. "Okay, can't wait to see it."

"Thank you for helping today." I squeezed his arm because, apparently, I had the desire to touch him and since I wasn't sure why he'd stopped hugging me, this seemed like the most appropriate form of physical contact I could get away with in the moment.

He squeezed my arm back in a joking manner. "You're welcome."

"Are you making fun of me?"

"I mean, sort of, yes."

I laughed.

Asher glanced back at the group. "Did you force Chad to come or what? He doesn't seem like he wants to be here."

"No, he was getting off work when I was picking up Bean. He asked. I figured we could use an extra body."

I studied Asher's face for a reaction, but there was none.

Bean became restless at my feet and tugged on the leash to head back to the table.

"Oh, now you want your drink?" I asked him. He smiled up at me. "If only you knew we were doing this all for you, you cute little jerk." I met Asher's eyes and nodded toward the others. "Should we . . . ?"

"Yeah." He lingered for a second longer, like he wanted to say something. But Bean was tugging my arm and instead Asher laughed at him and led the way back.

"Who won anyway?" Brett asked when Asher and I reached him.

"I think Bean did," Asher said.

"I think that dog lost big-time," Chad said. "Not sure there will be many prospects with that footage."

I bit my lip. He was probably right.

"The only loser today is my pants," Dale said.

That earned a laugh from Kamala.

"I heard they were expensive," Brett said.

Dale threw his empty doggie coffee cup at him.

"Will you AirDrop me the video?" I asked Kamala.

"Yes, of course." She pulled out her phone and pushed several buttons.

"Ooh, I want it too," Brett said.

Then everyone had their phones out and were accepting the video from her.

"Just don't post it anywhere," I said. "I have to mess with it." The whole point of this activity was to show Bean looking lovable. I had my work cut out for me.

"Yes, ma'am," Dale said.

"We better get Bean back to the shelter," I said. It closed at five on Saturdays and it was almost five.

"Bye, Wren," Asher said, squeezing my arm again, his eyes twinkling.

"You're such a punk."

CHAPTER 13

• • • • • • • • • • • • • •

Rule: *The only person who should give you*
butterflies is an entomologist.

I was curled up on the couch cradling my stomach when my dad walked in a little after seven o'clock. He was late.

"What's wrong?" he asked, hanging his keys, then sitting on the bench and unlacing his boots.

"I ate dairy a couple of hours ago and now it's rotting in my stomach refusing to come out."

He tucked his boots under the bench. "Why did you do that?"

"Because I'm an idiot."

He sat down next to me smelling of grease and sweat. He reached for my head like he was going to pat it, but he must've noticed the condition of his hands, lined with grime, because he dropped them into his lap instead. "Can I do anything for you?"

"When the time comes, just let me die. Don't resuscitate."

He chuckled. "Even in pain, your sarcasm can't be contained."

"Pain brings it out more, Dad."

"How was your day?" he asked. "Aside from the poisoning?"

"Can we adopt a really sweet dog? You would love him. Please, it's my dying wish." I'd been trying to edit the Bean Game footage since I got home but was having a hard time spinning it to make Bean look lovable. Probably another reason my stomach was hurting. Bean wasn't the only one who hadn't performed well. Between me spitting onto the grass, Chad's sour face, and Dale just staring in disgust at his drink before it was spilled all over his lap, it was a pretty underwhelming video. At this rate, we were never going to get Bean adopted.

"Wren, I'm allergic. If a customer brings a car into the shop that's had a dog in it I'm wheezing after thirty minutes."

"I could keep him in my room and vacuum every day."

My dad gave me his *I'm sorry* eyes. "Even if I weren't allergic, you'll be gone to college in a year and I work all day. A dog would be miserable here."

He was right, of course. I sighed.

"I'm sorry, kid."

"It's okay, I get it." I sighed again. "Why are you so late today?"

"A brake job I needed to finish."

"Sounds important."

"Hey," he said. "I don't mean to bring this up in your state, but have you talked to your sister in the last day or two?"

"No, why?"

"She's driving up to see Mom next weekend."

I ran my hand along the fabric of the couch cushion. "Yeah, Mom said."

His brows came together. "You got your mom's texts? She thought she must've still been blocked since you didn't respond."

"I was thinking about it."

"About responding?"

"About going."

"Going?" he asked, obviously surprised.

"Do you actually *want* me to go? Aren't you on my side? Shouldn't I stay home?"

"I'm on everyone's side," my dad said.

No! I wanted to scream, *You can't be on everyone's side.* "I was leaning toward no, actually," I said.

"Whatever you decide I will support, but it would be nice if your sister wasn't driving up there alone."

"Do it for Zoey? Is that the angle you're going with?" My stomach cramped and I pushed on it.

"It's up to you, kid."

"You won't be sad all by yourself on the Fourth of July?"

He laughed a little. "I'll manage. I need to shower now."

"You're not going to watch thirty minutes of TV?"

He looked at me lying on the couch that he normally had all to himself. "I'm really that predictable, aren't I?"

I put my thumb and forefinger as close together as possible without them touching. "Just a little."

He seemed to accept my very accurate assessment. "Do you want the heating pad for your stomach?"

"Death. I want death."

He left, and I texted Kamala. *Never let me look at dairy again.*

I clearly labeled your drink. I'm sorry you were trying to juggle two boys and forgot how to read.

There was no juggling. I closed my eyes and groaned.

Another text came in: *You don't have to use it.* Below the text was a link.

"Huh?" What was Kamala talking about? But then I saw the name across the top of my screen. Asher.

Butterflies fluttered to life in my stomach. "Nope, you should be dead in there with the rotting milk," I muttered.

This link isn't going to put a virus on my phone is it? I responded back.

No. Just follow it

Don't tell me what to do

My text was a joke, but I really did hate surprises and I had no idea what following that link would result in. I followed it anyway.

The video started with the words *The Bean Games* on a black screen and some sort of fight song playing in the background. The words shook and then shattered to reveal: *Can you best our beast?* Those words faded out to a shot of Dale's backyard and the table and participants. A voice-over rose above the music: "Meet today's lucky competitors. They are up for a chance to win a gift card from Meg's. But they have to beat our favorite shelter resident, Bean the Great." The voice lowered and said, "Currently up for adoption." Then a big photo of Bean's smiling face, the *Adopt Me* scarf around his neck, filled the screen. My face split into a smile. He was so cute.

The next bit played out exactly like I remembered it except with slow-motion sections and Asher calling it like a sporting event, complete with funny asides and descriptions of what everyone was doing, things like "Bean goes for the distraction technique with a tongue to his opponent's ear." When Bean ran across the table, me following (I honestly didn't remember being on the table), Asher closed with: "And that's how you win a competition. If you thought that looked fun, please comment below to be a future participant for a chance to win prizes and meet our favorite animals."

I watched the video through once more, then closed out of the screen. He'd done it—made the video look fun instead of a disaster and brought out Bean's personality, the one that only came out for certain people.

You're brilliant, I texted.

A second later, my phone rang. I hesitated, not really wanting to talk in my sick state, but I found myself answering. "I told you not to make that."

"Hello to you, too."

"Hi, that was really good."

"You don't have to use it," Asher said.

"I don't have to use the masterpiece? I can make my own mediocre version?"

"Correct."

I laughed. "I'm using it, but noting that you aren't a good listener."

"This is also true."

"Also, a gift card to Meg's?" I asked. "Where did that come from?"

"Since it was just us, I made it up. But I figure a little bribe wouldn't hurt to get people to sign up for the next one."

"Probably true," I said. "You have a good voice-over voice, by the way."

"Yeah?"

"Yes. Easy to listen to." My cheeks went pink with that state-ment, which was really annoying.

"Thank you."

"So how do I put this video on our page?" I asked.

"You can share the administrator password with me and I can put it on."

"Um . . . yeah, okay."

"Are you not allowed to?"

"Yeah, not really." I'd been asked not to share it when Erin gave it to me. But Asher had just put hours into this video. I knew he had. No matter how easy he said it would be.

"I can just give you my YouTube password and you can upload it yourself, if you'd rather," he said.

A large smile took over my face. *It's just a password, Wren, not his firstborn.* "I'm sure I would have no idea how to do that. I'll text you the password. But don't tell Erin I gave it to you. And don't post weird things on the page."

"Like doggie porn or something?"

"You did *not* just say that."

"I meant dogs, just dogs, not humans and—"

I let out a small scream. "Please! Stop while you're ahead. Your sweet, innocent image is evaporating."

"If it helps, my face is bright red right now."

I laughed. "That actually does help."

"Sometimes I speak before I think."

"You do? I hadn't noticed."

"You're not a very good liar."

I went quiet as he reminded me that yes, I actually was a good liar and I hated that.

I must've groaned because he asked, "What's wrong?"

"My stomach is bothering me. Dairy."

"Dairy?"

"Me and dairy don't get along."

"But . . ." He trailed off.

But what? What had I said? My mind spun as my stomach flipped.

"I thought you liked coffee with loads of cream. That's what I ordered you."

Right. Gemma. Stupid Gemma, always ruining it. "Yes, I do. For sure. I think it was expired or something." I hated myself.

"I'm sorry. If you're not feeling well, I'll let you go."

"No!" I blurted out. "I mean, it's nice talking to someone, it's a good distraction from the pain."

"Okay."

I sat up and hugged my knees to my chest. "What were you doing before you called?"

"Making a video about this dog at the local shelter."

"That sounds noble. Are you always a save-the-day kind of guy?"

"What does that mean?" Asher asked.

"I don't know why I'm asking. You totally are. I mean, you're doing all this for free. Erin says, be a volunteer. You say yes. Erin says, perform a miracle for this dog. You say, sign me up."

"You think I'm doing all this for Erin?" he said.

"Well, for Bean."

"You think I'm doing all this for Bean?"

My heart stuttered in my chest and then hammered to life twice as fast. "You shouldn't do anything for me," I said, my voice low.

"Why not?"

"I'll end up disappointing you," I got out in a relatively normal voice.

"How?"

"I'm closed off, private . . . broken." And apparently a huge liar too.

"Isn't everyone?"

I gave a breathy laugh. "Kamala isn't. She's very open and trusting. Seems to know exactly how things will play out and doesn't mind just letting them. You seem to be the same way."

"You think I can see the future?"

"More than I can." I wanted to see the future now. Like how would Asher react if I spit out the whole truth. Would he run away and never talk to me again? Or would he laugh it off? And what would Dale do? Still follow through with his humiliation plan? Fill Asher's head about how all this made me a horrible person? "Or maybe you just don't worry about it."

"The future?" he asked.

"Yes."

"I do," he said. "If I need to."

"I worry about it all the time. Analyze it. Try to bend it to my will."

"Does that work?"

"Sometimes," I said.

Asher hummed as though analyzing my statement. "What were *you* doing before I called?"

"Laying here on my couch groaning."

"Wren . . . I need to . . . there's this . . ."

"What?" I asked with a nervous laugh.

"What event should we do next week? For Bean, I mean?" he said, but that's not what he was going to say. None of his half starts made sense with that finish.

"I don't know," I said, giving him a pass for the moment. "Maybe we should see if anyone actually signs up before we plan another one."

"Did Chad get in your head?" he asked.

"No . . . sort of."

"He's kind of negative."

"He's realistic."

Asher let out a short grunt. "And you like that? Realism?"

"No." I paused, thinking about it. "Well, sometimes. I like to feel grounded and have reasonable expectations about things. That way I don't get disappointed."

"I'll try not to disappoint you, Wren," he said.

I swallowed, those stupid butterflies somehow surviving my apocalyptic stomach.

But what if I disappoint you?

CHAPTER 14

· · · · · · · · · · · · · · · ·

Rule: *Never change for anyone except your overly critical conscience.*

I banged on my sister's front door over and over. "Zoey! Hurry!"

She opened it with a bewildered look on her face.

"I have to pee!" I threw my stuff right inside the door and went tearing through her house to the bathroom down the hall. Its countertops were littered with makeup and hair utensils and scrunchies. I lifted the lid on the toilet to find a gross yellowish-brown water ring around the bowl.

"Blech," I said, and lined the seat with toilet paper like I did in public bathrooms. Zoey's house was closer to work than mine, so today I decided to use it like a pit stop. I didn't think it would actually look like one, though.

"Why didn't you go before leaving work?" Zoey asked when I came out.

"Because someone was in there and I wanted to leave. I thought I could make it home."

"Obviously not," she said.

"Your bathroom is gross."

"It's not my week to clean it, but I should probably go in there and straighten it up a bit."

"No, that's not what I was saying at all. You should make whoever's week it is do it."

She laughed a little. "I'm not the boss of the house. The toilet worked, right? That at least deserves a two-star review."

"That's a great idea, leave a sign by the door where people can rate their experience. Then maybe your roommates will be shamed into cleaning."

She rolled her eyes.

"Where are your roommates anyway?"

"Work. And Jasmine is taking a summer class." Zoey sat on the couch and I saw a show paused on the television. "Oh!" She held out her hand. "Let me see your phone."

"Where is *your* phone?"

She nodded across the room. "Plugged in. Let me see it."

I placed my phone in her hand and she opened the Instagram app and typed something into the search bar. Then she turned the phone toward me. "Who talked you into this? I need to know."

I squinted at my phone even though I already knew what she was referencing—the Bean Games video. I slid closer to her and pointed to Asher on the screen.

"Really? Olive Garden Boy?" She stared at the still image for a couple of beats. "Huh."

"What?"

"I just . . . you usually hate putting yourself on social media. You dumped a cup full of goo on your face."

"But look"—I pointed to the comments below—"people are signing up. We already have ten people for our next event and it's only been posted for three days."

"That's cool. I was just surprised to see you in the video."

Maybe Asher did bring out a different side of me. A better one. Maybe I *could* be a person who didn't have to know how things turned out before I committed to them. "I'm going to go with you to Mom's."

Zoey's mouth fell open and she shut it again. What I expected to see on her face, happiness, was not there. Only shock.

"Do you not want me to?" I suddenly wondered aloud.

"It's not that I don't want you to," she said, ever the peacemaker.

"It's beginning to feel like it is," I said, when she didn't go on.

"I want to have a good trip. I don't want you to come and be mean to Mom and for it to turn into a crappy weekend. I want to have fun. I haven't seen her in forever."

"Neither have I."

"You haven't wanted to," Zoey reminded me.

"True."

"But if you want to come and you'll call a truce for the weekend, I think it could be good. For all of us."

So not only was I going, I had to be nice too? Maybe it was time to give our mom a second chance (or third or fourth or whatever number we were on). Everyone wanted a relationship with their mom, I was no different. Plus, it would be nice to spend some time with Zoey. Ever since she moved out, I felt like we'd drifted a bit. "Okay," I said.

"Really?" *There* was the happy expression I had been waiting for.

I nodded.

"Sister trip! I'll make the playlist."

"I'll bring the snacks."

There was a buzzing sound. "You got a text," Zoey said, still holding my phone. She scanned the screen and read out loud, "Are we still on for tomorrow?"

"You're reading my text?"

"I was holding your phone, it was reflex." She had obviously read the name too because she said, "Asher? Is that Olive Garden Boy? What are you guys doing tomorrow?"

I honestly had no idea. I plucked my phone out of her hand and reread the text. The last time I had talked to Asher was when he called after sending the video. We hadn't made any plans. "I don't know."

Another text came through: *Invite Kamala because Dale wants to come. Is that okay?*

What time again?

Noon by the bay.

The bay? As in the ocean? I hoped he just wanted to sit and look at it because there was no way I was getting in the water, not even to uphold plans that Gemma had obviously made. *He's still messaging with her?* How? How was she pulling off pretending that she knew the things we had done? Was this someone he knew? Someone who had insider information? I had assumed he had stopped DMing her when he started texting with me, figuring we were one and the same, but he obviously hadn't.

130

I thought about texting back that something had come up. Work, or *something*. But Asher knew as well as I did that the shelter was closed on Wednesdays. And besides, I hadn't seen him in three days and I found that I really wanted to. Also, what if Gemma showed up this time? Decided to come clean. What if this was her do-over? Her chance to really meet him? I needed to be there to tell my side of the story.

CHAPTER 15

· · · · · · · · · · · · · ·

*Rule: If a guy wants you to go in the ocean, he
needs to provide the protective metal cage.*

"Do you think the real Gemma will show up today?" Kamala asked
as we sat on the beach towel I had spread out on the sand, still not
sure exactly what we were doing. Maybe we were going for a ride in
Dale's boat. I could handle that. In front of us was the rocky shore;
to our left a boardwalk ran along the water's edge lined with restaurants on the land side and boats of various shapes and sizes on the
water side. I didn't remember what Dale's boat looked like from
the one picture I'd seen on Instagram, but it could be one of those.

"I don't know." I'd been wondering the same thing the day
before.

"Would it be a relief at all?"

"If Gemma was real?"

"Yes," Kamala said.

My throat tightened and so did my chest. *What is that about?*

"He would pick you," she said.

"What? No, I still don't like him like that," I said. I *couldn't* like Asher like that. I'd been lying to him. This wasn't something I could just joke my way out of at this point. He would not choose me. He'd choose the person who had been truthful . . . or at least *more* truthful.

"Okay, whatever you say." Kamala's eyes caught on something over my shoulder and went wide. "Don't panic."

"What? What is it?" I asked, going perfectly still. "Is it a sea lion? Did one come up behind me?"

She rolled her eyes. "Seriously, Wren? Has that ever happened to you in the history of going to the beach?"

"There's a first time for everything." I looked over my shoulder, feeling a bit safer, and saw the real reason for her warning: Asher and Dale, heading our way from the parking lot of the closest restaurant, each holding a paddleboard under one arm.

"No," I said. "No, no, no, no. Why do they have those?"

"They are probably planning on paddleboarding," she said. "With us."

"Not happening." I felt the panic bubble rise up my chest at even the thought of going out there. "How am I going to get out of this? Help me think of a way out."

"There's this little thing I like to call the truth," Kamala said, smirking. "You open your mouth and the words that come out of it are things that are real."

"You want me to tell Asher I'm not Gemma right here, in front of Dale, the wannabe influencer."

"Dale is not some heartless troll."

"I mean . . ."

"Hello," Asher said as he and Dale joined us. "Where are your boards?"

"I was told you were an award-winning paddleboarder," Dale said. "I personally like my water sports to involve motors, but using my own muscles once in a while keeps them from atrophy."

Award winning? Was this girl the self-proclaimed best at *everything*? "Who told you that? Your masseuse?"

"I don't think my masseuse knows your paddleboarding history," he said.

"She meant the atrophy part of that statement," Kamala said.

"Oh," Dale responded. "The atrophy part was obviously fictitious." He flexed his biceps as if to prove his muscles were the opposite of withering.

"How are you?" Asher said to me. He looked adorable in his swim trunks and an oversized bucket hat.

Panicking! I wanted to yell. "Trying to figure out what we're going to do for the next Bean Games. We have twelve people signed up."

"I know! And Chad thought nobody would be interested."

"Who's Chad?" Dale asked.

"He was literally in your backyard," Kamala said.

"Oh, the pretty boy?"

"He *is* pretty," Kamala agreed.

Asher looked at me. "No comment," I said, and he laughed.

Dale dropped his board in the sand and slid a backpack off his back. He unzipped it and pulled out a helmet with some sort of bendy antenna on top. "Check it out," he said.

"What exactly are we looking at?" Kamala asked.

Dale took his phone out of the front pocket of his bag and attached it to the antenna. "We will capture it all out on the water."

"Have you never heard of a GoPro?" Kamala asked.

"Do you know how much better video quality is produced by my phone?"

"I guess not," she said.

"What exactly is there to capture out on the water?" I asked.

"So many possibilities. Did you ever see that video of the kayaker swallowed by the whale?"

"Yes!" I responded, pointing to Kamala.

"Ugh," Kamala said with an eye roll. "Don't get her started."

Dale slid the helmet onto his head.

"You look like an idiot," Asher said.

"Says the guy in the bucket hat."

"Is that . . . ?" Dale was staring at something behind me.

I screamed and whirled around.

"Elinor?" Dale finished, and I let out a relieved breath until I processed what he'd actually said.

My eyes zeroed in on every single person, one at a time, in the parking lot: an old man with a beard, a woman holding hands with a toddler, an Asian girl around our age with long black hair and perfect skin. She wore a bikini top and shorts and she was gorgeous.

"Wren thinks a sea lion is going to sneak up behind her and what?" Kamala said in my direction. "Eat you?"

I forced my eyes away from Parking Lot Girl who may or may not have been Elinor and pointed to Dale's helmet. "Remember that video of the sea lion who pulled the little girl off the pier and into the water?"

"That won't happen," Kamala said.

"I actually saw that video," Dale said. "I hope that *does* happen."

"Sea lions are tools," Asher said. We had an inside joke and I hated that I liked that.

"What's she doing here, dude?" Dale asked, not one to be easily sidetracked.

So it *was* Elinor.

"I don't know," Asher said. "There's only one bay in town and it's not like I own it."

"I should ask my parents to buy it. Then we *would* own it."

Asher sighed and Dale laughed. I rolled my eyes but laughed as well. He really was doing it on purpose, making himself seem more obnoxious than he was. I could see that now.

Kamala looked confused. "Who are we talking about?"

"My ex," Asher said, gesturing toward the parking lot like Elinor was still standing there. She wasn't. She had gone into one of the restaurants along the dock. Or I assumed she had, because I couldn't see her anywhere.

"Your ex showed up today?" Kamala caught my eye. I knew what she was thinking. Was Elinor Asher's catfish? Had she been trying to meet him today? A weird play to get him back or to get back at him?

"So, seriously," Asher said, changing the subject, "why didn't you bring your boards?"

"They're locked in her sister's garage," Kamala said, surprising me. I didn't think she was ready to perjure herself for me, but maybe she had gotten a glimpse of the girl in the parking lot too and was second-guessing her declaration earlier that Asher would choose me. Maybe she decided with that one look, that he wouldn't. "She borrowed them and now she's at work."

"We can rent some from the place on Main," Asher suggested.

"No, we can take turns on these," Kamala said, grabbing hold of Dale's wrist. "We'll go first."

I wanted to hug her, but instead I dropped back onto the towel and tried to gain the feeling back in my legs.

CHAPTER 16

· · · · · · · · · · · · · · ·

Rule: Most games worth playing have boundaries.
Don't date a guy who doesn't have any.

"Have you ever taken any of the dogs from the shelter paddle-boarding?" Asher asked. He'd spread a towel out and was sitting next to me.

"No. We should've brought Bean. Got that on video." Before he asked me any more questions about my paddleboarding history I flipped it to him. "Have you ever taken your dog?"

"No, my mom thinks Buffy's too little and that the creatures of the deep will eat her."

"Smart mom."

He laughed like I was joking.

I dug my sunblock out of my bag and applied some to my arms. "Are you okay, by the way?"

"Why wouldn't I be?"

I nodded behind us, to where his ex-girlfriend had been fifteen minutes ago.

"Oh yeah. It was weird. I haven't seen her since school got out. It just surprised me. I don't . . . There's no leftover feelings or anything."

I raised my eyebrows, moving on to my legs with the lotion.

"Okay, no leftover *good* feelings."

"What happened? You said she broke up with you, but why?"

He took a moment with that question, as if thinking about how to summarize the downfall of a relationship in one sentence. "She wanted more of me, I think."

"You're so open, though. How many layers did she want?"

"What I mean is, she wanted me more to herself."

I put a quarter-sized dollop of lotion in my hands, rubbed them together, and applied the sunblock to my face. "Oh, she thinks you share yourself with too many people?"

"Yeah, probably," Asher said thoughtfully. "That's a good way to put it."

We had the opposite problems. I shared myself with next to nobody.

"Well, share myself in the non-prostitute way," he clarified.

I gave a breathy chuckle. "You only do it for free?"

His eyes went wide and then he let out a large laugh. "Exactly."

"Is it all rubbed in?" I asked, facing him. "The sunblock?"

He studied my face for what felt like an eternity and then reached out and ran a finger along my temple. "Now it is."

My cheeks were pink. I looked up at the sky like the sun was the culprit.

"Do you want me to get your back?" he asked.

One finger along my temple had set my face on fire. I couldn't imagine what his hands on my back would do. I turned anyway, passing him the sunblock over my shoulder. *You can't like him, Wren, you are living a lie.*

I stared out at the glistening water in front of us. A girl on a sailboat unfurled the sail, revealing large colorful fabric. Asher's hands ran along my back, strong but gentle, massaging the lotion in. I hugged my knees to my chest. "I *like* how open you are," I said. "It's rare. It's nice."

"*You're* nice," he said.

"I'm really not."

"You have me fooled."

"I think I do," I said.

He finished, capped the lotion, and tossed it onto the towel. I turned back toward him. His cheeks looked a little pink now too, but maybe it was just the blasted sun. I stole his hat off his head, freeing his beautiful mess of auburn hair, and put it on mine.

"That looks cute on you," he said, leaning back on one elbow.

He poked my side and I giggled, a rare occurrence for me. I dropped down to my elbows so we were more level. I wanted to tell him who I was, or more accurately, who I wasn't. Why did I want to tell him so bad and yet was so scared to do just that?

"Do you need some sunblock?" I asked.

His eyes dropped to the bottle between us and then back to me. He swallowed and then nodded, turning his back to me. I sat up and took a deep breath. Had I ever applied sunblock to another person in my life? Sometimes I'd use the spray kind on my sister's back, but this seemed different. It *was* different. I squeezed way too much sunblock into my hand. Asher's back was hot; the sun had been beating down on it for the past fifteen minutes or so. I pushed his hat, which was still on my head, up with the back of my wrist so I could see better. I ran my hands along his back and he shivered, then laughed.

"Sorry," I said.

"No, it's, no . . ."

Something cold and slimy landed on my leg and I looked down to see a long green squirming thing. I screamed, kicking and pushing it off, a dark memory pulling at the corners of my mind.

A loud laugh rang out.

"It's just seaweed," I heard a calm voice say. "Wren."

"What?" My eyes locked with Asher's.

"It's off."

"It's off," I repeated, my heart beating in my throat.

Dale and Kamala were walking toward us with their boards. Dale had obviously slung that piece of seaweed on me. He was still laughing that obnoxious laugh of his, the one that had motivated me to start this whole lie to begin with. He was wearing his helmet with the antenna on top and looked like the biggest goof.

"You okay?" Asher asked.

I nodded.

"Your turn," Dale said, dropping his board in front of us, water and sand splattering onto my legs.

Oh, right. No, I wasn't okay. "You're a jerk," I said, kicking the seaweed in his direction.

"Yes, I am."

Asher got up right away and grabbed his board. I stared at the one I was supposed to use like the enemy it was.

Kamala plopped down beside me. "Look," she said in a low voice. "I didn't even get wet."

"But you've done it before," I responded in a voice equally as low. There was leftover sunblock on my hands and I wiped them along my legs.

"Show us how it's done," Dale said. "Paddleboard master."

"And apparently," I directed to Kamala, "Gemma is really good at it."

"You have to face this fear sometime."

"But do I?" I asked.

Asher was heading toward the water, already several feet away from us, and he looked at me over his shoulder with that smile of his. "You coming?"

"I'm going to pick up this board and walk to the water and when I get there you are going to get some call about something that we must leave immediately for," I said quickly and quietly to Kamala.

"You're going to drag me into this?" she asked.

"You are all the way in it, girl."

She smiled and gave me a shove. "Fine. Go."

I snatched up the board and paddle and rushed to catch up to Asher. He was already ankle-deep in water. "It's cold," he said when I was next to him.

The jetty separating the bay from the open ocean eliminated the waves, but the water still lapped at the shore in tiny ripples.

I zeroed in on the water, which became darker and more opaque the deeper it got.

"You look pale," Asher said, the water now up to his calves.

"I'm pretty white."

He chuckled.

I strained, listening for Kamala to rescue me, but so far nothing.

Asher laid his board across the shallow water and attached the strap around one ankle. "You can't make fun of me for my lack of coordination."

I set my board down in front of his. *Come on, Kamala.* "I won't."

Asher walked behind me and attached my leg strap as well. When he stood, he cussed under his breath.

My heart jumped, but I didn't see any danger, besides what was lurking in the depths. "What?"

"Incoming."

I turned just in time to see the girl from the parking lot pass Dale and Kamala, heading for us. Dale immediately ripped his phone off its makeshift helmet stand and followed her, obviously recording. He really thought he was a reality TV star. Did people care about his day-to-day life as much as he thought they did?

"Asher," Elinor said when she stood in front of us. She was shorter than she had looked from a distance. "I thought that was you."

"Hi," he said, friendly as always. "How are you?"

"I'm okay. We just got back from San Diego."

"Visiting your sister?" he asked.

"Yes. She had her baby. A little boy—Ezra."

"Oh wow. Congratulations."

"Thanks." Elinor's eyes flitted to me.

Asher noticed and took a step sideways, angling his body in front of me in a protective way. "We were just about to go out on the water," he said. "Nice seeing you."

"You're not going to introduce me?" she asked.

"I'm his girlfriend," I said, reaching out and slipping my hand into Asher's. "Wren. Nice to meet you."

Elinor couldn't hide her shock for a brief moment. Her eyes locked on our linked hands, but then she tamed her expression to neutral.

I tried to read her reaction. Was she just shocked because she hadn't seen Asher since school got out and his having a new girl-friend was surprising news? Or was she shocked because she had been talking to him online as Gemma and had no idea his relation-ship with the person who had stepped into that role in real life had progressed this far?

"Hi, nice to meet you," she said. "I didn't realize . . . I had no . . . How did you two meet?"

Crap. Here it was. If she was Gemma she could call me out right now. Before Asher could say anything, I said, "In a coffee shop." Because that *was* where we met.

Elinor narrowed her eyes. "Wait, are you—"

"You don't know her," Asher said, not realizing he was saving me from having to answer any more questions that might expose my lie. Or hers. If she *had* been lying to him online.

"Wren!" Kamala called. "Your phone is ringing! Do you want me to answer it?"

She was following through with her promise to get me out of becoming a floating bait trap, but the timing wasn't right. Did she not see that? I couldn't leave now. Not with Elinor here—she would probably ask more questions as soon as I was gone. I gave Kamala a thumbs-up, hoping she'd interpret it correctly.

"We met online first," Asher was saying.

"Yeah . . ." I stepped back, my body apparently trying to get out of this conversation, and I tripped over his leg strap, or maybe mine. Then, as I tried to catch myself, my heel caught on the board behind me that was floating in the shallow water. My other foot stepped right on top of the board. It went out from under me and I fell backward, onto the second board. It, too, was not stable and between my momentum and the shifting boards, I tumbled off and right into the water.

I landed on my back and immediately went under. The water was cold and all the air was sucked from my lungs. My feet were still up on the board, but my entire torso and head were underwater. I thrashed, trying to bring my head above water or to free my feet. Blackness closed in on me. A bed of seaweed tangled around me, pulling me deeper. No, that was a memory. That wasn't happening. I could feel the bottom. The bottom was right there. I pushed on it and sat up.

My head broke the surface and I coughed and gasped for air. Asher was at my side, kneeling in the water, his hand on my back. Had he helped me up?

"Are you okay?" he asked.

I nodded even though I really wasn't. "I just need to stand. Get me out of here." My cheeks were as hot as the surface of the sun.

Asher helped me to my feet as his ex-girlfriend watched.

"Please let me put that on TikTok," Dale said.

My eyes whipped over to Dale, whom I had forgotten about. "If you do, I will cut you up in little pieces and feed you to the sharks."

Asher laughed.

"Ugh. You're no fun," Dale said.

"Hi, Dale," Elinor said.

"Hey, witch."

Sometime in the midst of the chaos, Kamala had joined the group. She was holding out my phone. "It's your boss."

I shook my head at her, hoping she'd realize I needed like five more minutes.

"No, really," Kamala said. "It's *really* Erin. She needs to talk to you."

Water was dripping down the back of my neck and off my chin and down my legs. I walked toward Kami but was stopped short by the ankle strap, which was still on my leg. Kamala closed the distance and handed me the phone.

"Hello." My teeth started to chatter, from being cold or from the shock of what had just happened. I squatted and untethered myself from the board. "You still there?"

"I'm so sorry," was how Erin answered. "I didn't want to bother you on your day off, but you are my fourth call. Everyone is out of town or not answering."

"What's wrong?" I asked.

"The cameras are showing a drop-off at the front of the shelter. You think you could go check it out? I'm three hours away." A drop-off was when someone left an animal, usually in a box, at the shelter doors after hours.

"Yes, of course."

"Thank you so much."

"No problem," I said.

"Will you call me back with a report?"

"I will." I ended the call. "I have to go."

Asher looked between Elinor and me like she was the reason I was fleeing. She was actually the only reason I probably needed to stay. But I had to go and hope that Asher would let me explain later if Elinor outed me. If she really was Gemma.

I pointed to Dale. "Don't post that video."

He gave me an innocent shrug, but I didn't have time to threaten him more. I'd have to trust that he was just jerk-like on the surface like Asher kept telling me.

I reached my towel, shook it off, and wrapped it around me. When I picked up my beach tote I remembered that Kamala had driven us here. I turned around to see where she was and nearly collided with Asher.

"Do you really have to leave or was that a staged emergency exit?" he asked. Dale and Kamala were right behind him.

"That was Erin. We had a drop-off at the shelter."

"I'm coming with you," Asher said, abandoning the board he held. "I can drive."

"I'll give Dale a ride home," Kamala offered.

My eyes found Elinor, still lingering by the water. "Okay, let's go."

CHAPTER 17

· · · · · · · · · · · · · · · ·

Rule: *Always date a good hugger.*

It had turned into a windy day and as Asher and I approached the cardboard box in front of the shelter, the flaps were slapping open and closed with each gust. I pulled the towel I still wore tight around me with a shiver.

"Maybe it's just a delivery?" Asher said. He was still in his swimsuit as well, but he'd thrown a T-shirt on. We did not look like shelter employees on official business. We looked like beach bums, sandy feet and all.

"It's not a sealed box."

"True."

I peeled back one flap revealing a crumpled blanket. I carefully lifted the blanket to find three tiny kittens. They were very quiet and mostly still. I touched one gently. It was colder than it should've been, which worried me. I entered the code on the shelter's front door and the lock slid open.

"Will you grab the box?" I asked, turning to Asher.

He was already holding it, securing the bottom with one hand.

"Thanks," I said.

"Of course."

The shelter felt different after hours, empty of humans. It felt colder, darker, even less homey than during regular hours. The ever-present barking still filled the air. I led Asher toward the medical room, flipping on lights as I went. "It's okay," I said as we passed kennels, the dogs getting even louder. "Just me."

We walked down the aisle and to the far corner, where the medical room was. Once inside, with the door shut behind us, I called Erin and filled her in. She gave me instructions on where the formula and heating pads were and what to do.

"Is this just a day in the life of Wren?" Asher asked after we had managed to give each kitten a syringe full of formula and they were resting comfortably on a warm pad in a crate.

"Oh yes," I said. "Very typical."

Asher sat on one of the tall stools, his elbows on the counter, as he peered into the crate. His hair was flopping over one eye, and he wore a cute smile as he stared at the tiny kittens.

"You are adorable," I said.

"Are you talking to the kittens or me?" he asked.

"Definitely the kittens."

"I *am* pretty cute," he said.

"Will you watch them for a minute?"

"Yes, for sure."

I left the room and beelined for Bean, greeting other dogs as I went. Bean was lying on his cot. I stopped in front of the chain-link gate and he stood up and stretched. I let myself inside and sat against the brick wall closest to the gate, not sure what surprises would be toward the back. Bean walked up to me and lay beside my leg, putting his head on my thigh. I scratched him behind the ears.

"Hey, boy. How are you?"

He let out a long whine.

"That good, huh? We're working on it, I promise. What would you like to do for your second challenge? We have twelve partici-pants ready." My butt was still wet from the ocean and I was sure I was leaving a nice mark on the cement. "You like to be wet. What about a swimming race?"

My mind took me back to earlier, the feeling of being trapped under the water. My breath caught in my chest. Bean inched for-ward and put his head under my chin, calming me. "You're a good boy. I won't make you go in the ocean. What about a pool? You think the community pool would let us host a competition there?"

He licked my hand.

"I think so too."

Barks echoed off the stone, and I leaned my head back against the wall. "I'm sorry you don't ever get any real peace, Bean. I'd be grumpy too if I couldn't get a good night's sleep . . . for nine months." Bean nudged my hand and I petted his head some more.

"I left a boy in the other room I should probably get back to," I told him. "That's a whole different story. I called myself his girlfriend today to another girl. It was to help him, he knew that.

He won't hold me to it. I don't want him to, right?" I remembered the feel of Asher's back under my hands and my pulse quickened. "I know how you feel about him, so you're way too biased to give any opinions about this. He doesn't even know me. Or he thinks half of me is a whole different person. That's probably the half he's drawn to. Because the other half . . . the real half is just closed off and full of rules." I sighed. "I better go." I gave Bean one last rub and stood up. He stood as well. "I don't work tomorrow, but I'll see you the day after, okay?"

I hated leaving all the animals here, but I especially hated leaving Bean, knowing it had been such a long time since he'd had a family, someone he could see every day and trust. It's probably why he gave trust so sparingly. "I completely understand," I whispered as I latched the gate and headed back to the medical room.

When I let myself in, Asher was still sitting on the stool but now he was staring at his phone.

"How is Bean?" he asked.

"How did you know I went to see Bean?"

"Just a hunch."

I shrugged. "He seemed okay."

"We'll find him a home soon. Look at all the attention he's getting and we only did one event."

"I hope you're right."

"Are we supposed to feed them again?" Asher turned his phone toward me. "Google says every two hours, but they didn't get a lot in the first feeding."

"You've been Googling kitten care?" I asked.

"How old do you think they are?" He swiped a finger down his screen. "It says the younger they are, the harder it is for them to survive without their mom."

"They'll be okay. They seem tough." My voice cracked, followed by stinging eyes. *Seriously?* I cleared my throat.

Asher's eyes shot up to mine.

I held up my finger toward him. "It's nothing. Don't read into it."

"What happened today? Out there in the ocean?" he asked, like he was the most insightful boy in the world.

I let out a huff of air. "I said not to read into it."

"I read into everything."

"Everything? That's *my* job." I walked to the counter and put the lid on the can of kitten formula, then slid it back on the shelf.

"So?" Why did he make it so easy to talk with his relaxed posture and nonjudgmental expression?

"When I was a kid I nearly drowned in the ocean. A lifeguard saved me. My mom was on the beach. She got distracted."

"Distracted?"

"I was old enough to swim. It wasn't like I was a toddler," I said, surprised by my need to defend my mom. I didn't normally feel that way. "I just went out too far, got tangled in seaweed, or caught in a riptide, or both. I don't know. I couldn't get back to shore and I tired myself out." I leaned back against the counter, my legs weak with the memory of kicking until I couldn't anymore. Of floating down beneath the surface before the strong hands of the lifeguard grabbed hold and pulled me up.

We don't need to tell your dad what happened, she'd told me as we drove home. *It will just worry him.*

"I was fine. I *am* fine. I'm not some helpless kitten."

Asher gave a small warm laugh, then stood and walked over to me. He put his hands on the counter on either side of me. "You are not helpless at all, but I'm sorry that happened. It sounds scary."

I tugged on the hem on the bottom of his T-shirt, my eyes down, staring hard at the thread running the length of it. "Why are you so likable?"

"Why do you sound mad about that?"

Because I didn't know how he'd feel once he learned I'd been lying to him. And it sucked that I cared. I was very aware of the fact that now I had something to lose. I didn't need more things to lose.

"You know if you're *not* fine, that's okay. You can talk to me." he said. "I'm probably not as good of a listener as Bean, but I actually talk back."

"Bean talks back. He's practically a therapist."

Asher smiled that adorable smile of his.

"Wait, did you hear me out there?" I nodded toward the door.

"No, I swear."

I sighed and ever so slowly leaned forward until my forehead touched his shoulder and my chest was against his. His arms encircled me and I closed my eyes. Yes, I needed him to get back in the habit of hugging me because *this* made everything better.

CHAPTER 18

· · · · · · · · · · · · · ·

Rule: *Always date a boy everyone loves.*

Kamala was spraying down tables in the coffee shop and wiping them with a rag. I sat at a table in the nook.

"Did you paint that on the window?" I pointed to the beach scene.

"Don't make fun of it."

Did everyone think I was judging them all the time? I hoped not. "I wasn't going to! It's good. I was going to say it's good. I didn't know you painted."

"I don't. It was a do and learn–type situation."

"You should add it to your résumé."

Kamala narrowed her eyes at me and pointed the dirty rag in my direction. "I can't tell if you're being sarcastic or not, but I'm just going to say thank you."

"I'm not sarcastic *all* the time."

"Most of the time," she said.

"Well, not this time, so there."

The bell rang as the front door opened. Becky and Meredith, two girls from school, walked in.

"Hey, Kamala, I didn't know you still worked here," Becky said.

"She paints the window now too," I said.

Kamala rolled her eyes in my direction as she walked to the counter and both the girls studied the window painting like a hidden message was there.

Meredith was the first to look away and begin her drink order. After, she turned to me. "I almost didn't see you over there."

"Yes, that's why I like this corner," I said, pointing to the bookcases and oversized counter plant.

"I saw you online," she said.

Kamala laughed, probably thinking Meredith's comment was karma for my painting comment.

"Oh yes," I said. "It was messy but fun."

"Yes, it seemed like it. It's getting lots of views."

"We're doing another event tomorrow at the pool," I said. "You should come. Bring friends."

"Another video?" Becky asked, after paying.

"Yes."

"So are they staged?"

"I mean, we set them up and then whatever happens, happens."

Becky nodded. "Nice."

"Yeah . . . ," I said, not sure what else to say.

Kamala was fast with their drinks and they waved goodbye as they left.

"The rec center is going to let you use their pool for the Bean Games, then?" Kamala asked.

"Yes, I talked to them this morning."

"It's crazy how many people have seen that video. That's good for Bean."

"I know," I said with a smile. "Asher's brilliant with social media. Seriously, the shelter should hire him just for that."

"Why would they hire him when they're getting him for free?"

"I know, I feel bad."

"He's a big boy," Kamala assured me. "If he didn't want to, he wouldn't."

"True."

"Speaking of, have you found any of his social media yet?" she asked. "He obviously has it."

"No, I keep waiting for him to like a post on the shelter's page, but he hasn't. At least I don't think he has."

My phone buzzed with a text. A picture of the kittens came on my screen. *Guess where I am?* Asher wrote.

Lucky, I texted back. *Are they doing okay?*

So good

Good. After the emotions of last night wore off, I was super embarrassed about how I had reacted in front of Asher. He'd given me that charity hug after sensing I was on the verge of tears and I'd held on to him for an awkwardly long time. Long enough for him to realize I was more upset than I was letting on. And that made me angry. My mom didn't get to have this effect on me anymore. I'd spent years crying over her.

In the middle of that eternal hug, Erin had showed up, saving Asher. I'd lain in bed the rest of the night analyzing the day. I'd called myself his girlfriend to Elinor, then made him comfort me through a breakdown.

My phone buzzed again, bringing me back into this moment, in the café with Kamala. A selfie of Asher and Chad popped up.

Chad's working today? I texted.

Yes, I've decided he's actually pretty cool.

"I overstepped yesterday," I said, turning my phone toward Kamala.

She leaned over the counter to get a closer look. "What does that have to do with overstepping?"

"Asher is trying to show me that he just wants to be friends. Not only that, he's friends with everyone. Even the guy he thought I might've liked."

"Huh?"

"He wants me to know that he's a friend to all. That he would rub Chad's back if Chad was upset." Yes, at some point during our forever hug, Asher had begun rubbing my back.

"Oh please," Kamala said. "Now who's being dramatic? Stop reading into that picture and focus on the fact that he's texting you pictures. He wants to talk to you."

"He wants to talk to everyone."

"You know what your problem is?" Kamala asked.

"Which one? I have many."

"You feel like you revealed too much last night. You like this boy. You showed him more than you were ready to show him and now you're pretending like it's him who's trying to pull back when really it's you."

I stood and went to the lit display of baked goods by the register.

"You know I'm right!" Kamala said.

"You know what my main problem is? Aside from what you just said." Which was probably true as well. "I lied to him. No good relationship starts with a lie. We were screwed from day one."

"Well, yeah. Like I've been saying, this thing was a ticking time bomb to begin with."

"You were supposed to disagree with me," I said.

"Why would I do that?"

"Because I like him," I whined.

Kamala's eyebrows popped up. "You're finally admitting that out loud. To me. What about Chad?"

"My brain liked him."

"Your brain is the worst," she said.

"It really is."

She slid open the glass door of the display case, picked out a big chocolate chip cookie, placed it on a napkin, and handed it to me.

"I'm *this* pathetic?"

"Yes, eat away your sorrows."

I took a bite, chewed, then swallowed. "So . . . is there any way at all I can get away with not telling Asher about the catfishing thing?"

"Nope." Kamala gave me her sad look. "But, Wren, you always had good intentions. You were doing it to help him. It might not blow up as bad as you're imagining. And if he likes you too—"

"*If,*" I interrupted.

"You don't think he does?"

I closed my eyes. "I don't know. I think he liked Gemma. And he really does seem to get along with everyone. He's just so nice. Right? Do you think he's nice?"

She gave me a half smile and a nod. "He's very nice."

"Exactly!" I said through a mouthful of cookie. "Maybe everyone thinks they're special when he's around. Day one he gave me the world's best hug. If he's going around handing out hugs like that, every person in his life is in love with him."

"Are we back on Elinor again?"

"Yes! Including her." That was another thing Kamala and I had talked about when I arrived at the café—what had happened with Elinor after Asher and I left the bay. Apparently, she had wandered over to Dale and begun riddling him with questions. To my surprise, Kamala said he defended me, telling Elinor I was cool and that she should leave Asher alone. *This means he's not suspicious of you anymore, Wren,* Kamala had said. *This means you can tell Asher about the whole catfish thing and not have to worry Dale will humiliate him.*

Maybe it did mean that, but I was still terrified.

"I'm sorry that more than your brain actually likes a boy. It's not a fun feeling to let your heart out of its cage, is it?"

I took another bite of the cookie. "It sucks. And it's only out for loan."

"Your heart?"

"Yes, I'm just letting him borrow it for a while. It's a trial run."

Kamala laughed. "If that makes you feel better."

CHAPTER 19

· · · · · · · · · · · · · ·

Rule: Always date a boy who loves animals.

Kamala raised her eyebrows at me as I walked into the rec center with Chad, who had tagged along again when I went to pick up Bean. She was probably thinking this wasn't a good way to send Asher the message that I liked him. She was right. I was terrified to send him that message.

She was on the far side of the pool talking to Asher. He was showing her angles or lighting or something while pointing his phone at the pool. The rec center was muggy and smelled like chlorine, but right now, it was still relatively empty. We had an hour before the event was supposed to start. Bean was pulling against his leash, ready to jump in the water immediately.

"You have to save your swimming for the audience," My voice was louder than I intended, echoing off the tiled walls and floors.

Asher looked up, met my eyes, and smiled. My stomach clenched. I wanted to be next to him. I wanted to run over there

160

and give him a hug. But I also wanted to wrap myself in armor and never let him in.

"What do you need me to do?" Chad asked.

"I think Kamala is going to be filming it. I'll start Bean on that side of the pool with the contestants."

"Should I stand on this side of the pool and call to him once it starts?"

"I'm going to have Asher do that. Bean really likes Asher."

"Most do, it seems," Chad said. He sounded bitter.

"You don't?" I asked.

"I don't know. Someone that nice has got to be hiding something, right?"

I laughed. "You're almost as skeptical as I am."

"I can be," he said.

I looked around the room. Bleachers were set up on one side of the pool. I pointed. "Maybe you can be crowd control? I'm guessing people aside from the contestants are going to show up. Let's keep them over there, contained on the bleachers. I don't want Bean to get too distracted."

"Sounds good. Did you bring towels or anything?"

"The center provided some, I think." A folded stack sat on the edge of the pool. "There."

"I can be on towel duty too."

"That works. Thanks for helping, by the way."

"Of course. This should be entertaining."

"I hope so." I looked down at Bean. "You'll be entertaining, right?"

He gave me a happy bark.

"He said yes," I informed Chad.

"Of course he did."

Movement across the pool caught my eye. Asher and Kamala were heading our way. My cheeks were going red. They really had a mind of their own lately. I squatted down and began petting Bean. "This is it, boy. I feel good about today."

He licked my face.

Asher arrived and I was still down by Bean.

"Hey, guys," he said. He held his fist out for Chad, who bumped it half-heartedly. "I didn't know you were coming today."

"Yeah," Chad said. "I came for Wren."

Well, that sounded loaded. I bit my lip and looked up. "We ran into each other at the shelter. His shift was over."

Kamala nodded as if that answered any questions she might have had when Chad and I walked in together.

"You guys got here early," I said.

"I just got here," Kamala said. "Right before you. I don't know how long he's been here." She glanced over at Asher.

"Not long," he said. "I was too excited to stay at home any longer." He squatted down next to me and greeted Bean. "Hey, boy. You ready for today?" Bean's tail went crazy. "Everyone is going to love you."

Asher and I were shoulder to shoulder and he looked at me. "It's been a couple of days. How are you?" he asked in a soft voice.

"Good, so much gooder. Better. I'm better. Than last time, I mean. Last time was . . . it was whatever."

"I'm glad you're gooder," he said with a smirk.

I nudged his shoulder with mine. "How are you?"

"The goodest."

"You like to make fun of me."

A smile stretched across his adorable face. "I really do."

I stood. Asher did as well. Bean seemed to finally notice Kamala and he snorted at her.

"Rude," she said.

Chad laughed.

"Let's go over how this is going to work," I said.

The participants stood, lined up along the edge of the pool, waiting for the countdown. Some were wearing goggles and even swim caps. Some were wearing their everyday casual clothes and looked like they had wandered in off the street. There were about fifteen who were going to swim. But those fifteen had brought friends and family members to watch. Half of Asher's family had come and were holding up signs that said *Go Bean!* and *Attaboy!*

Asher's mom had stopped by to say hi when they first arrived and gave me a hug. I wished I had let Asher hug me earlier instead of talking to Bean to avoid him and my red cheeks and my insecure thoughts.

I was nervous, my heart beating fast, as I stood next to the contestants with Bean, the noise of the spectators echoing all around us. Bean seemed a bit nervous too, and that wasn't helping either.

The rec center director walked over to Asher, who was on the far side of the pool. I'd told Asher to talk to him because, of course,

Bean found him suspicious when I tried to have a conversation with him earlier. So I was now keeping Bean away from the director so that the contestants didn't see what a punk he was. Asher said something that made the director laugh. Then Asher caught my eye and mouthed, *You got this.*

Could he really see my nerves from that far away?

I nodded. It would be fine.

The director cleared his throat. "Welcome, everyone, to this canine race." The audience went quiet. "Our pool is open all year and we hope you'll consider us for your aquatic needs. My co-director, Sally, over there is ready with membership applications if you're interested after the event."

Sally, a redhead holding a clipboard by the bleachers, raised her hand.

"But for now," the director said, "let's do some swimming. Remember, the winner earns a free oil change from Niles's Auto Shop. And if Bean wins, he gets a free oil change." Everyone laughed.

I rolled my eyes. As if my dad's boss offering a free oil change would make up for years of underpaying him.

The director held his hand in the air. "Contestants ready?"

Several loud cheers sounded.

He dropped his hand and yelled, "Go!"

All fifteen people jumped in the pool. But Bean, who had been itching to get in the water earlier, just stood staring at it, like his whole future didn't depend on looking fun and adorable right now.

"Come on, Bean. Go! Go!" I said.

He looked up at me as if asking why in the world he would do that.

"You can do it!" I said, pretending I was about to jump in, fully clothed. Bean called my bluff, staring up at me, seeming to say, *You think I'm stupid, don't you?*

Then, as if to show me what he thought the pool was for, he lifted his leg and sent a stream of pee over the edge. The audience groaned.

Someone from the bleachers yelled out, "It's not a great color! He probably needs to drink more water!"

Loud laughter followed.

I wanted to melt into the ground from embarrassment.

Bean barked in the direction of the rowdy crowd as if defending himself.

"Seriously, Bean?" I was tempted to pick him up by the handle of his doggie life jacket and drop him in. But I would never do that. He had to choose to jump on his own.

A chant of "Go, Bean, go!" started in the bleacher section where Asher's family sat.

"Look, they're beating you," I said, pointing to the people, who were halfway across the pool now. Right as I said it, a body streaked by me and crashed into the water with a loud splash. When the person surfaced, hair matted to his face, I saw it was Asher.

"That's cold," he said. Then to Bean, "Come here, Good Boy!"

Bean gave a happy bark and went flying, landing in a belly flop next to Asher. The audience laughed and clapped. And then Bean and Asher swam side by side the length of the pool. When Bean climbed out on the other end, I rushed around to join him. He walked into the middle of the group of contestants who had already finished and sprayed water all over them with a shake. Then he barked at each of them and took off running when someone reached down to try to pet him.

Asher, who had just joined me, his wet shoulder bumping into mine, said, "He really wants us to get our cardio today." With that, he reached for my hand, a questioning tilt to his head. "Are you with me?"

CHAPTER 20

. . . .

Rule: *Never pee on your future.*

"I feel like this is going to be your pep talk after every event. *Don't worry, I'll fix it in editing,*" I said as Asher and I sat poolside.

After I had taken his hand, we chased Bean twice around the pool before Asher's family stepped in to help. That's when he'd dropped my hand. I wasn't sure if it was to corner Bean more effectively or if it was because his family had surrounded us. Once Bean was finally settled at our feet, Asher and I dried him with several towels while chatting with Asher's mom and sister.

Eventually, everyone filed out, only a few people giving Bean a tentative goodbye on their way.

"I *will* fix it in editing," Asher assured me, leaning back on his palms and looking out across the still water of the pool.

"Will you edit Bean as well?" I asked. "Make him a dog who doesn't pee on his future."

"I think we all pee on our future sometimes."

I lowered my brow at him and he laughed.

"I thought that would sound deep, but it really didn't."

"No, it didn't," I said. "But thank you. For editing again. Are you sure?"

"Yes, I'm sure. You said I was a genius last time, so you'd be stupid not to use me."

"I believe I called you brilliant."

"Same thing." He bumped my shoulder with his and I wiped at the wet mark he left behind. "Where did Kamala go?"

"She had to work," I said. Chad was on the other end of the pool, talking to the rec center director. I wasn't sure what he was saying. I didn't think a single person had signed up to join the center. "I drove Chad here." Why had I done that? Sitting next to Asher, all I wanted to do now was spend the rest of the afternoon with him.

"Cool," Asher said. Did he mean that?

"But can we, can I, can we see each other later?"

The puddle that had formed around Asher from his wet clothes was spreading closer to me. I scooted back.

"Are you afraid of a little water, Wren?" he asked, inching closer.

I laughed. "Yes, I don't want to get wet." I backed up again.

"What? You don't want to get wet?" He jumped to his feet.

"Don't you dare," I said, ready to run.

He launched himself forward and I only got off the ground and two steps before he wrapped his arms around me from behind.

"Ew!" I squealed. "You're so wet!" I screamed it while at the same time relaxing back against him. Even soaking wet, Asher's arms felt good around me. Was I the perfect size for his arms or was he just the perfect hugger? I wanted to think it was the first one, that we fit just right together.

"You are very warm," he said next to my ear.

"Are you cold?" I asked. "I can't believe you jumped in with your shoes on."

"Sometimes I do impulsive things, stupid things," he said.

I stiffened at those words. They were the ones (along with many others) I used to describe my mother. I knew Asher was a free spirit, impulsive, someone who could hurt me.

"What's wrong?"

"Nothing . . . I . . . um . . . thanks for jumping."

"You were stressed and I wanted Bean to jump." His words reminded me of something he'd said on the phone a while back. That he was doing these things for me. Which reminded me of what Chad had said earlier: that *he* had come here for me. My eyes shot over to Chad, who was now staring at us. I took a step forward, out of Asher's arms.

Then I turned to face him. I needed to tell him the truth so we could get out from under this cloud that hung over us, ready to burst. "Can we . . . talk later? After I drop Bean and Chad off?"

"That sounds serious," Asher said, his brows drawing low in faux concern. "We definitely shouldn't be having serious conversations while I'm soaking wet."

Bean was lying on a pile of towels to our right, obviously exhausted from the excitement. A discarded sign lay on the ground next to him. It read: *Get Wet for a Cause!*

"Your family's?" I asked, pointing to the sign.

"Probably," Asher said. He peeled off his wet sweatshirt. He had a T-shirt on, which was equally soaked and stuck to his toned chest. He shook his head and water droplets hit my face. He smiled. Why was he so adorable? Why was I going to ruin everything with my confession later?

"Excuse me," a woman to my right said. I hadn't even heard her approach. "Have you seen a pair of red goggles?"

"No, I—"

"Is she looking for goggles?" Chad called from across the room, holding up a pair and proving he was paying even more attention to me and Asher than I had realized.

Behind the woman a little girl, probably eight or nine, stood staring at Bean, who had sat up at the sight of the new visitors.

"Thank you!" the woman called, and headed toward Chad.

The little girl lingered, she and Bean in an eye lock.

She inched forward and I started to move as well, but Asher flexed his fingers toward me as if saying, *Just give them one second.* Bean's tail was wagging and we were close, so I did.

"Hi, Bean," the little girl said. "You're so cute."

Bean's mouth stretched into a doggie smile. He and the girl finally met. They were inches from each other when Bean reached up and licked her face from chin to forehead. She laughed and scratched his head.

I looked at Asher. He was watching the exchange with the biggest smile on his face.

"Maggie, step back!" called the woman, who now held her goggles and was coming back toward us, Chad beside her.

"It's fine, Mama! He's nice!"

Bean licked the little girl's face again and I laughed. Once the woman reached us she took Maggie's hand and pulled her several feet away from Bean. My chest tightened and I prayed to the dog gods that Bean would like Maggie's mom as much as he liked Maggie. But Bean, being who he was, seemed to think now was a good time to walk in slow tight circles, as though he was chasing his tail, but much less playful and much more weird. The woman stared at him for a few moments, then said, "Uh, thanks. Good luck." She walked away, hand in hand with the girl.

"I love him," Maggie said as they left.

"He loved you, too!" Asher called after her.

The woman didn't look back.

"That was so close," I said, disappointment settling onto my shoulders. Bean had stopped spinning and his smile from before was gone. I picked up his leash from the ground and clipped it to his collar. I scratched behind his ears and kissed his face.

"If we just had to convince kids," Chad said, "there wouldn't be any dogs in the shelter."

Asher met my eyes. "It was close."

"You ready?" Chad asked me, like we were a couple or something.

"Yes." I said. Asher had never answered my question about getting together later. Did that mean he didn't want to? "Bye."

"I'll walk with you guys." Asher's shoes squeaked and left watery footprints as he walked.

"Thank you so much!" I called to the rec center director, who waved.

"You really should've had Bean on leash with that little girl," Chad said, in a careful voice.

He was right. I should've. We had rules for a reason.

"He was fine," Asher said. "His body language was relaxed and friendly."

"It's policy," Chad said.

"You're right. I will next time," I said.

We reached my car where Asher paused. "We'll talk later, yeah?" he asked. So he *did* want to see me later?

I nodded, and he and his wet shoes and dripping sweatshirt walked to his car.

Chad buckled Bean in and then we both climbed into my car. After a few moments of driving in silence, Chad said, "Are you still going to Tahoe for the Fourth?"

"Oh yeah, I am." I had forgotten he was going there too.

"We'll have to meet up."

"Yeah, I'm not sure what my schedule will be, but maybe." Maybe my sister would enjoy a party with people our own age. Maybe I'd need a break from my mom. Maybe the confession I was about to make to Asher would blow up in my face and I'd need lots of distractions over the coming week.

CHAPTER 21

· · · · · · · · · · · · · · ·

Rule: *The truth will set you free . . . hopefully.*

I sat in my car in front of Asher's house. It had been less than thirty minutes since we left the rec center. I still wasn't sure if he actually wanted to see me. He'd said *see you later*. That wasn't necessarily a planned meeting. It was a common departure phrase. But I was determined to get everything out in the open. Now that I'd admitted out loud I liked him, it was time to get this weight off my shoulders and put it all out there.

The blue front door looked extra bright today. A big potted plant sat to the right of the doormat and Asher's wet shoes were to the left.

I knocked before I talked myself out of it. Buffy immediately started barking.

His mom answered, holding Buffy, and seemed surprised to see me. "Wren! I didn't know you were coming over." She gave me a side hug, which confirmed to me that Asher was just a hugger, like his mom. It was genetic or something. "That was so fun today. Bean is just the sweetest."

"He really is," I said. "Even when he's being a total punk."

She laughed. "I wish we could adopt him, but Buffy doesn't like other animals." She bounced Buffy in her arms. "Huh, you little snob, you like to be the only princess around here." She opened the door wider. "Come in. I believe Asher is in the shower, but I'll go check."

"Thank you. Should I . . . ?" I pointed to the show couches.

"Oh, honey, we don't sit on those."

I smiled. "Why would you?"

"You can wait in Asher's room. He gets dressed in the bathroom."

"Okay, cool."

Only his mom was wrong. Or maybe today was different due to the fact that he had been soaking wet when he came home, because he walked into his room several minutes after I did in just a towel. His lanky body was toned and tan and my cheeks went red.

He let out a strangled yelp when he saw me and then laughed.

"I'm so sorry," I said, rushing for the door. "Your mom told me to wait in here."

"I usually get dressed in the bathroom," he said.

"I know. I mean, I know because she told me, not because I've been spying on you or anything."

His eyes twinkled.

"I'll wait in the room with the fancy couches that I can't sit on," I said, practically running out of the room and closing the door behind me. I heard him laughing on my way down the hall.

When he finally joined me, dressed, he was still chuckling. "You really wanted to see me later. Like, all of me."

"Funny." I shifted from one foot to the other several times.

"You don't need to be embarrassed," he said, taking my nerves for embarrassment (which was a safe bet, I was that too). "I was wearing a towel. You've already seen me in my supershort swim trunks."

I wanted to flirt back, if that's what this was, but I couldn't. The weight of the lie on my back was getting heavier by the second. "Do you want me to be here?"

"What?" Asher asked.

"Right now? Should I leave? I can leave."

He took a step closer but that was all, just a step. "No. I mean, yes, I want you here. Why wouldn't I?"

"You used to hug me more," I blurted.

He smiled. "Do you need a hug?"

"No. I mean, yes, but no." I couldn't hug him now if I could never do it again after today.

"What?" He put one hand on my shoulder. "What's going on?"

"Would Dale really embarrass you at his party if he found out you were being catfished?"

Asher stared at the wall behind me thoughtfully, as if a scene was playing there. "Have you ever done something to help someone even if it didn't necessarily help you?"

"No . . . ," I started, but that was a lie, wasn't it? That's what I had done in the café weeks ago. "Yes. But I don't understand . . . how would getting humiliated help anyone?"

He shrugged. "Dale likes to make videos. I don't mind looking like a fool."

"I wasn't trying to make you look like a fool," I said. "When I . . ."

He nodded encouragingly, almost like he knew what I was going to say next. My knees felt wobbly. We should've gone back to his room so we could sit down. Instead we both stood there by the fancy couches and I blurted out, "I need to tell you something."

"Me too," he said.

"I'm not your catfish," I said, not really processing what he had said. "I mean . . . you were getting catfished. Maybe. I don't know, maybe Gemma was really Gemma, but Gemma is not me and I'm not her and . . ."

"You are not each other?" he finished for me.

"Right. I tried to tell you in the car weeks ago."

"I know," he said.

"You know?" Now I was confused. "Which part?"

"All of it. I've been trying to tell you that too."

My mouth opened and shut. "Why didn't you?"

"Probably the same reason you didn't tell me."

Why hadn't I told him? "Because you felt sorry for me?"

He let out a single laugh. "Okay, not the same reason. You felt sorry for me?"

"I mean, that's why I pretended to be Gemma that day in the café. Dale was making fun of you and threatening to humiliate you and you looked so . . ."

"Pathetic?"

"No, not pathetic. Sad. It wasn't supposed to last this long. I was going to tell you right away that I wasn't her. I just wanted Dale to see that you could've been talking to—"

"A hot girl?"

"No, just *that* girl. Whoever you were really talking to. Who were you really talking to?"

"I have no idea. She refused to meet with me. Meaning she probably wasn't the person she was claiming to be. Or maybe she's just really shy. I don't know."

"But you knew it wasn't me?"

He smiled. "Yes. You knew nothing we had talked about online. Plus, your name tag kind of gave you away at the shelter."

"So why didn't *you* tell *me*?" I asked.

"Because I wanted to *keep* talking to you. I wanted to get to know you. Maybe I thought I needed an excuse." He drew in a breath. "Are you mad?"

The weight that had been sitting on my shoulders for weeks was gone, leaving me feeling light and giddy. I was relieved, surprised, confused, but not mad. How could I be mad when I'd been doing the same thing? "No. Are you?"

Asher shook his head.

"But wait . . . D&D?" My eyes widened. "Paddleboarding? I thought *she* made those dates with you."

He held his hands up. "I had no idea you were scared of the ocean. None. And D&D was just funny. I knew you didn't know how to play. I thought you'd confess. You didn't confess."

"I need to sit down," I said. After all those weeks of worrying and dreading this admission, it all seemed too easy. I'd been waiting for a fallout. This didn't feel like a fallout.

"Yes, sit down." Asher gestured to the couches.

I sank to the floor instead.

He smiled and dropped down next to me.

"I'm going to buy your mom plastic couch covers," I said. "My grandma had some and they worked wonders. They make couches usable."

He reached out his hand, palm up.

There is nothing between you now, no more excuses, my heart said. *That's why you're scared, that's why you think there's still a fallout coming, you're trying to protect yourself.* "I like you too much," I said out loud.

"You like me too much to hold my hand?" Asher asked.

"Yes."

"You've never liked anyone before?" he asked.

"I thought I did, but it didn't feel like this."

"How does it feel?"

"Scary," I admitted.

"You're scared of me?"

"I'm scared of getting too attached and then losing you. I'm scared that maybe you're not careful with your decisions. That you just fly into them headfirst."

He slowly ran a finger down my arm. "Has this felt like a fast progression to you? Because it's felt like the slowest buildup I've ever experienced in my life."

I laughed. "I may be a little closed off. You know, the whole *mom abandoning me* thing. I know, I know, everyone talks about how well adjusted I am, but it's a front."

"Oh yes," he said, playing along. "I just heard someone say that a few days ago. *That Wren, she's so well adjusted.*"

"You mean when I was having a breakdown at the shelter?"

"You call that a breakdown?" he asked. "It could use some work."

"I'm a notorious underachiever."

Asher inched closer to me. "You know what else they said, those nameless people? They said Wren doesn't use humor for deflection at all."

"They were right." I hugged my knees to my chest.

He inched even closer, stretching one of his legs out behind my back and sliding the other leg under my bent knees. "What if," he said, "you stay in your bubble of protection and I climb in there with you?"

"I think there might be room," I said, my shoulder against his chest now.

He wrapped one arm around my back and the other joined my arms around my knees. I let myself relax against him.

"Are *you* scared?" I asked softly.

"Terrified."

We locked eyes. His were gorgeous and sincere, just like he was. "Has anyone ever told you that you're the world's best hugger?"

"If I say yes, will you still want to kiss me?"

"Who says I want to kiss you?"

"Your eyes are telling me, Wren. Finally."

"Then why aren't you kissing me?" I asked.

"Because you're still deflecting."

I stretched up and pressed my lips against his, my hands grabbing hold of his shoulders. His lips were soft and full, and an immediate buzz of pleasure crawled up my spine.

Asher gasped in surprise, like I'd caught him off guard.

I pulled back. "I thought you were expecting that."

"I assumed you needed a few more rounds of sarcastic deflection first."

"You must be the one who needs that," I said.

He shook his head twice, then his lips were on mine again. His hand left my knees and found its way to my waist, bringing me closer. I shifted to face him and he pulled me onto his lap, deepening the kiss. My skin was hot yet covered in goose bumps. We both moved to our knees and then our feet and then he was lowering me onto a couch, all while kissing me. I tried to protest our new seating arrangement, but with his lips on mine, and his thumb circling the exposed skin on my side, I found I didn't care. My brain hadn't been this empty and my skin hadn't been this tingly in a long time.

"You're even better at kissing than hugging," I said between kisses.

"Nobody has told me that before," Asher said, smiling against my lips.

"Good. You're no longer allowed to kiss anyone else."

"I only want to kiss you."

"Asher Jordan Linden," Asher's mom said, coming into the room. We pulled apart. "What are you doing?"

I knew she wasn't asking about the make-out session she had walked in on. She was worried about me defiling her couch, not her son.

"We're sitting, Mom," he said.

"We are now standing." I stood and pulled Asher up by his arm.

Cori smiled. "I know I'm ridiculous, but these were my mother's couches."

"They're very pretty," I said.

After she left the room, I asked, "When did your grandmother pass away?"

"She didn't. She moved to Florida."

I laughed. "I should probably go. I didn't tell my dad I was going anywhere after the rec center."

Asher tugged on my arm, pulling me against him. "But the D&D group is coming over. You said you'd play."

I gasped and hit his chest. "You are the worst."

He wrapped his arms around me. "But you still like me."

"Yes, I do." I stepped out of his hug and led him by the hand toward the door.

"I'm going to walk my girlfriend out," he called to his mom. Then to me he said playfully, "Am I allowed to use the title you gave yourself the other day?"

"Only if you want to."

He nodded. "I want to."

"Bye, Cori!" I called.

"Bye, sweetie."

At my car, Asher pulled me into a hug. It felt even better than before. How was that possible?

When he pulled away I leaned my back against the car door. "I hope we can thank your catfish one day for getting us together."

"He or she or they is one of my favorite people now." Asher put his hands on the car on either side of me.

"You really have no idea who it is?" I took a fistful of his shirt and pulled him closer.

"None."

In the back of my mind I still wondered if it was Elinor. But right now, I didn't care. I wrapped my arms around his waist. And kissed him.

CHAPTER 22

· · · · · · · · · · · · · ·

Rule: *Always be proud of who you're dating.*

Asher was coming to my house this time and I felt the need to scrub every square inch of it. It was mostly my space, after all. My dad was hardly home and I couldn't blame messes on my sister even though she did leave them sometimes.

After cleaning the hall bathroom and kitchen I stood in my room and looked around as if I were the one who'd be walking into it for the first time. Asher's room was so full of personality, with its posters and paint. Mine was boring. What did it even say about me? The walls were white. I had a few Polaroids of Kamala and me around the mirror. My bedding was from my childhood. Like, literally, my mom had helped me pick it out when I was ten. It was blue with flowers on it. "Asher is not coming in here," I said to my bed. "You're very disappointing." I was going to get new bedding tomorrow.

I looked in the mirror, ran my fingers through my hair, then shut my bedroom door tight as I left.

It had been two days since Asher and I had kissed. Yesterday he had been busy with family stuff, but we were supposed to see each other today. Any minute now. I smiled.

A sound from the porch stopped me short as I walked down the hall, my heart jumping in excitement. But then I heard the front door open and close. Asher wouldn't just let himself in. Well, he might. That actually seemed like something he would do.

"Hello?" I called out as I walked toward the living room.

"Hey," Zoey said, heading for the kitchen. "Do you guys have any food?" She went to the pantry and stood there with the door open, sighing. "This is sad."

"I know," I said. I used to be so good about keeping to my weekly shopping schedule, but lately I'd been off, letting things like that go, realizing I didn't have to be so strict in my life with everything.

Zoey moved to the fridge and repeated the sentiment. Then she saw the chips and salsa I had put out on the counter for Asher and me.

"No, that's not for you." I pulled her by the back of her shirt. It did not slow her down at all. She just squealed and leaned forward.

"You're going to eat all of this?" she asked.

"No, I have a friend coming over."

"And you can't share?" She opened the bag of chips.

I smacked a chip out of her hand and she laughed. She slid onto a barstool at the counter, settling in and eating my chips. "Is this seriously all we have?"

"All *we* have. Me and Dad."

She threw a chip and it bounced off my forehead. "Ooh, what about the road-trip snacks you bought. Where are they?"

I wiped at the bit of salt the chip had left on my forehead. "I haven't bought them yet."

"You haven't bought them yet? We're leaving first thing in the morning."

"First thing in the morning?" I said, my brain slowly clicking through the calendar. "Oh wow."

"You forgot?"

"I didn't forget. I remembered we were going, of course. I just forgot what day it was." I'd been a little preoccupied kissing a boy. When Zoey gave me a look, I added, "It's summer!"

"I'm used to you being the controlling one. For once I get to be the big sister and remind *you* of something?"

I opened my mouth to respond when the doorbell rang. I held up my finger. "Stop eating my food," I said, and whirled around to get the door.

Zoey followed me, holding the bag of chips. "Kamala will share with me."

I stopped two steps from the door. "It's not Kamala," I breathed.

"Oh really."

Three more knocks sounded and seemed to echo through the house. "I don't need help answering the door."

"I'm curious who you're putting snacks out for and why you're all makeup-upped."

"You need to start calling before you come over."

Zoey smiled. "Then you need to start calling before you use my bathroom on your way home from work."

I braced myself and opened the door. Asher stood there in all his tall, lanky glory, looking super adorable with his floppy auburn hair and glasses. "Hi." He stepped forward as if he was going to give me a hug.

I turned toward my sister and said, "Asher, this is Zoey, my sister."

"Hi," Asher said, dropping his arms to his sides.

"Ah, aren't you Olive Garden guy?" Zoey said.

"I'm not their spokesperson or anything, but they make a mean lasagna."

"I guess these are for you." Zoey held out the bag of chips.

Asher took it warily. "Thank you?"

"Come in," I said to him. He stepped all the way inside and I shut the door.

Zoey just stood there like she was joining in on whatever we had planned. "Does Dad know you're having a *friend* over?"

"Seriously?" I said. "Do you want me to pull up the list of rules you've broken over the years and read it to Dad?"

She tilted her head. "I don't think I've broken any. Do you really have a list?"

"No, I don't have a list. That was supposed to scare you."

She laughed. "You should ask Wren about her dating list, Asher."

He raised his eyebrows at me.

"You shouldn't." To my sister I said, "I'm never telling you anything again."

"Am I not allowed to be here?" Asher asked, still hovering by the door.

"No, you're allowed," I said at the same time Zoey said, "No, you're not."

I took Asher's hand and pulled him farther into the room. "When did you turn into an old lady?" I asked my sister.

"I think I've always leaned toward old life. Buffets and jigsaw puzzles? Sign me up."

"I'm mostly looking forward to chair volleyball and golf carts," Asher said.

"Solid choices," Zoey responded. "Okay, I like him." But even with those words she didn't leave. I had a choice now: my sister or my embarrassing bedroom? I clenched my teeth and led Asher to my room, where I shut the door on Zoey.

Asher looked at me, his smile from when he arrived only half as bright now.

"I'm sorry, Zoey just showed up," I said.

"It's fine. She seems nice."

"She is. Too nice."

He extended the bag of chips.

"Oh, sorry." I took them from him. "Are you hungry? I have salsa."

"I'm okay for now."

I set the chips on my dresser and sat down on my childish comforter. Asher glanced around my boring room, then joined me, sitting what felt like a mile away.

Was this how relationships worked? Taking steps forward and then back again? I looked at the space between us and opened my mouth to ask him why he was so far away when he turned toward me and said, "I've been thinking about Bean."

"Okay . . ."

"We should lean into his less-than-lovable personality," Asher said.

"Um, what?"

He shifted his legs so he was completely facing me now. "Our strategy isn't working. We're trying to make Bean come off as some superfriendly *come play with me and fall in love*–type dog, but he's not. The videos are drawing people in, but Bean is not delivering once they're there."

"Right."

"So we lean into the fact that he doesn't like everyone. We make it a competition."

"Does Bean like *you*?" I said, catching on. "Come see if you're one of the chosen few."

"Exactly!"

"Yes, I like that."

"It's good, right?" Asher said.

"Have I ever told you that you're brilliant?"

"You have, actually. And I liked it very much."

I smiled. "Then why are you sitting way over there?"

He glanced toward the closed door. "Oh, I thought we were friends today."

I cringed. I'd hurt his feelings. I could see it on his face. He'd told his whole family about me for weeks now and was quick to call me his girlfriend to his mom the other day. And I hadn't said anything about him to my family. "I'm sorry. My sister and I don't share a lot of personal things."

"Why not?"

"I don't know. She tells our mom everything, so I kind of censor what I say to her. And she doesn't share much with me because I think she thinks I'm judging her."

"Are you?"

"Yeah, probably. It bothers me that she is so loyal to our mom after everything she's done."

"I understand that."

"You and Brett are close, right? How do you do it?"

"I share things with him. Even things he might not agree with."

I gasped in faux shock. "You want me to share things with people?" I slid across the mattress, closing the space between us and held out my hand, palm up. He placed his hand into mine.

"I'm going out of town tomorrow to see my mom," I said.

"Whoa. Really?"

"For the Fourth."

"Did you just learn about this today?" Asher asked.

"No, I decided last week, but I must've been blocking it out of my mind because I literally didn't remember it was tomorrow until my sister told me just now."

"You don't want to go?"

"Weirdly, I kind of do. I mean, that's why I'm going. I blame you."

"Me?" he asked.

"You've put me in a good mood lately. You're making me do things I don't normally do."

He laughed. "Don't give me all the credit. You have pretty good instincts."

I gave a breathy laugh. "Because I like you?"

"Because those instincts lead you to do kind things. Like help a pathetic guy in a coffee shop who you think is getting roasted by his friend. If your kind heart is leading you to visit your mom, maybe it's time."

I slid closer and he moved his knee, which had been between us, toward the headboard. I scooted into the space he'd created and snaked my arms under his, laying my head against his chest. He pulled on the ends of my hair and rested his cheek on the top of my head.

"Hold on one second," I said.

He nodded.

I stood and opened my door. "Zoey!" I called out.

"Yeah!" she answered.

"Asher is my boyfriend!"

"Okay, cool!" Zoey yelled back.

I shut the door and resumed my position. "Look at me, sharing things with my sister. I feel closer to her already."

Asher's chuckle vibrated against my cheek. "Nice blanket, by the way." He patted one of the flowers.

"Shut up."

"Tell me about these dating rules of yours."

"All you need to know is that I've broken almost all of them for you."

"That's because you're a rebel," he said.

I laughed. "Actually, it's because I feel different around you. You make me want to be more open."

"That's called trust," he said.

"Is that what that is? Huh." I squeezed his knee. "You also make me feel slightly off-balance."

"That's called lust," he whispered.

I smirked. "I could get used to it."

"I could get used to it too." He kissed me, one hand cradling the back of my neck. "You're very kissable."

"Kissable?"

"Yes, I want to kiss you *all the time*," Asher said.

"Then why did you stop?"

He chuckled again and pressed his lips against mine.

CHAPTER 23

· · · · · · · · · · · · · · ·

Rule: *Always date a boy who would sleep in a
chicken coop for you.*

"Can I borrow a pair of flip-flops?" Zoey asked the second she
came through the door the next day. "I forgot mine."

"We can just go back by your house on our way out of town if
you want," I said.

"Okay, fine, I lost mine. I can't find them anywhere. And
yes, I know if I cleaned my closet I would be able to find them
easier."

"I didn't say a word." I rolled my suitcase toward the door.
"There's a pair in my closet, top row of the shoe rack, third
space over."

"You have your shoe rack memorized?"

"The power of organization," I sang as I opened the front door.

Dad came rushing down the hall in his coveralls and socks.
"Don't leave without saying bye."

"I wasn't leaving, just loading the car."

He intercepted me and took over rolling my suitcase down the walkway to where Zoey had parked. "You'll be back Monday?" he asked.

"Yes, want me to FaceTime you the fireworks show Saturday night?"

"Don't worry about me, just enjoy yourself."

But I did worry about him, all the time. "I'll try," I said.

Zoey came out holding a pair of black flip-flops. "Found them. It was hard, but I managed."

"Funny," I said.

Dad lifted my suitcase into the trunk next to Zoey's. "Text me when you get there, please." He hugged me and kissed the top of my head, then repeated the action with my sister.

"Where are your shoes?" Zoey asked him.

"Under the bench by the front door," I answered for him.

Our dad smiled. "Apparently I'm predictable."

"Everyone knows that, Dad," Zoey said.

"Drive safe," he said.

I flung my backpack of snacks onto the floor of the passenger side, then climbed in.

Dad waved to us from the front porch as we drove away.

"You're okay, right?" Zoey asked. "You'll be nice to Mom?"

I rolled my eyes. "Yes, I'll be on my best behavior, Boss Lady."

"Was that an example of things you *won't* say?"

I pulled a bag of gummy bears out of my backpack and threw one at her head.

She laughed.

"Is this what a commune is?" I asked as we turned onto a dirt road lined with small houses and RVs and tents. A big garden and a firepit were to the left, in what looked like a common area. "Does Mom live in a commune?"

"I don't know," Zoey said softly. For the first time today she sounded wary.

For some reason, I wasn't surprised. This was exactly the kind of place I pictured our mom living.

She pointed at my phone. "Will you call her? Maybe we made a wrong turn."

I dialed our mom and listened to the phone ring.

"Hello," she answered.

"I think we're here. How do we know which one of these tiny houses is yours?"

"I'm the bus toward the back. I'll come out."

"She's the—"

"I heard," my sister said. She continued forward, slowly, as if delaying our arrival would make this place different by the time we got there. It didn't. We stopped in front of a literal bus at the end of the road. Its sides and windows were covered in murals of bright colors. It had no wheels, but it had a wood porch. Our mom stood on that porch with a smile. She looked exactly like I remembered and yet not. Older, less put together.

Pine trees surrounded the bus. The whole commune was in the middle of a forest. She had loads of potted plants on her porch and I was surprised to see they were thriving.

Our mom smiled as we climbed out of the car. "Girls! You made it!"

"Hi," I said, because my sister's voice seemed to have been sucked out of her.

"Look at you, Bird! You're growing up fast. You look just like me. Doesn't she look exactly like me, Zoey?" our mom said.

The words bit only a little, and I managed to keep my response, about how growing only seemed fast when you didn't see someone very much, to myself.

"Sort of," my sister said, walking around to the trunk.

"Your flowers are pretty," I said, pointing to the pots.

"Aren't they great? I don't have to do much. They're watered by the sky."

"The sky is good at that," I said, then sucked in my lips, wondering if Zoey would think that was an insult, considering the story I'd told her about Mom letting the farmers' market seeds die from lack of water.

Zoey didn't seem to be following the conversation at all. She was still taking in the bus. "Is this where we're staying, Mom?"

"This is my house, so yes! You'll love it. It's bigger than it looks."

"It'll be fine," I said, and actually meant it. I collected my suitcase. "It's only a few nights."

Zoey dragged her suitcase out of the trunk and it thumped heavily to the ground.

"Or were you planning to stay for months?" I joked. "What did you pack?"

She didn't laugh. Okay, she was in a bad mood. Noted. We did just drive five hours only to arrive at Tiny House Village.

We walked up the steps to the porch. Mom opened her arms for Zoey, who stepped into them and gave her a big hug. When it was my turn, I shifted sideways, giving her a side hug. It was more than I had thought I'd offer and definitely the most I could at the moment.

The part of the bus that normally had a folding bus door had an actual house door and our mom opened it and welcomed us inside. It was long and narrow, like a . . . bus. A living room was at the front, followed by a kitchen. There was a closed door at the back that I assumed was the bedroom. A shelf ran around the entire interior above the windows, and on that shelf were rocks and crystals of all different shapes and sizes.

"We should've brought backpacks," I said, noting that our suitcases were too big for the space.

"Where are we sleeping?" Zoey asked.

"Those two couches fold down into beds."

I hefted my suitcase onto one. "Dibs," I said, just to be funny. I really didn't care which couch I slept on.

"We didn't bring bedding," Zoey said. "Do you have any?"

"Oh yes, I have a lot on my bed. I'll gather it later."

I could tell Zoey was having some sort of mental struggle that I wasn't. Not that she'd actually say that out loud to our mom. Maybe I'd come into this with fewer expectations than she had. I wanted to reach out and pat her arm or tell her she'd be okay, but I didn't want to make it worse.

"I thought we could go pick some veggies from the community garden and make dinner together. And then tomorrow, I wanted to take you to the lake. I have a kayak," Mom said.

"Wren won't swim in the lake," Zoey said.

"I'll swim in the lake," I said. "It's the ocean I have issues with."

"You have issues with the ocean?" she asked. "Why?"

I looked at her. I wanted to yell, *Because you almost let me drown there, Mom.* But I had promised my sister I'd play nice and so far I was killing it . . . mostly. "Sharks, for one," I said. "Jellyfish, whales, octopuses, eels, urchins, fire coral . . . oh, and sea lions."

Mom was silent for a moment, then burst out laughing.

After a full day at the lake the next day and stopping at a few shops in town, where I got Asher a fun gift, I sat on the couch trying to think of the perfect way to word the Instagram post Asher and I had talked about a few days ago. Zoey and Mom were in the garden with several other community members. I had bypassed that immediately.

So far the trip had been better than I expected. I mean, our mom was still our mom—spontaneous, loud-laughing, oblivious to things outside herself—but she also seemed to be trying and I was glad for that. My sister's mood had improved after the initial shock on our arrival.

I squinted at my phone.

"Will Bean like you? Are you cool enough for Bean?"

Help! I texted Asher.

Mom issues?

Oh no, those are standard, and actually, things are going well. I'm trying to think of an Instagram post for the shelter. Will Bean love you or hate you?

Do you have what it takes to be the chosen one?

I typed back: *Yes! I like it.*

I think it was your suggestion when we initially talked about this. But also, you should get a stock photo of King Arthur pulling Excalibur out of the stone.

Will the average person know your old-school reference?

You obviously knew it, Asher pointed out.

Are you calling me average?

Never!

We're sleeping on a bus, btw.

Um . . . what?

My mom lives on a bus in this hippie commune. It's very much my mom.

Facetime me later with a tour? he asked.

I pushed the video button at the top of the screen and it started ringing immediately.

"Or now," Asher said when his cute face appeared.

"Hi, I miss you."

He smiled big. "I miss you, too."

"What have you been doing all day?" I asked.

"Not much, my mom dragged me all over town to help with chores."

"Such a good son."

"I mean . . ." He shrugged. "Are you going to post today about Bean?"

"The sooner the better, right?"

"For sure." His eyes looked around, taking in the bus and all its clutter. "What about you? What have you been doing?"

I pointed at my nose, which was a bit sunkissed from our time outside. "We went to the lake today and then into town, where we shopped for a bit. I got you a present."

"What is it?" He tried to peer around me.

"Why would I tell you that? But don't expect a lot. It's small and silly."

"I like small and silly," he said. "It's my favorite, in fact."

"Good, then you'll love it."

The front door opened and Mom and Zoey walked in with a basketful of vegetables and dirty hands.

"I better go," I said.

"Is that Olive Garden Boy?" Zoey sang.

"You know his name," I retorted.

"Who's Olive Garden Boy?" Mom asked.

"Her boyfriend."

"Does he work at Olive Garden?" Mom asked.

I turned my phone. "That's my mom."

"Hi, Wren's mom," Asher said.

She set the basket of veggies on the counter and walked closer. "Well, aren't you a cutie. You should've come to visit me."

"There's no room here for another person," I said.

"I have friends," Mom said. "We could've put him with the chicken guy."

I turned the phone back to me. "You hear that? You could've stayed in a chicken coop."

Asher shrugged. "I'd be fine sleeping in a chicken coop."

199

My mom laughed. "Not *with* the chickens. With the guy who keeps the chickens."

"Run," I whispered to Asher. "I'll talk to you later."

He smiled. "Bye."

We hung up and I went to the kitchen to help wash veggies.

"He seems nice," Mom said. "But you're too young to have a boyfriend. You have a life to live."

I did not take parental advice from someone who hadn't been my parent in a long time. "I'm living it," I said.

"Mom," Zoey said, probably worried that if we continued down this path, I wouldn't be able to hold my tongue, "are you going to come down for my graduation in May?"

"May? That's ten months away."

Zoey freed a knife from the block on the counter. "I know, I'm giving you plenty of notice. And do you remember Lisa? You used to work with her? She loves you. She's offering an internship at the hospital over spring break. You think you could call her and put in a good word for me?"

Our mom's face seemed to darken a shade as if the thought of actual responsibilities was too much for her to handle. My sister, cutting up a squash, was oblivious to the change in her demeanor. "You should come *here* for spring break. You have the rest of your life to work," Mom said

"It should be fun, Mom," Zoey said. "And it will be good for me to get to know some people there."

"So fun," our mom said with a loud laugh. What she didn't say was that she'd call or come down for graduation. My sister just smiled, not seeming to notice the omission as she added the squash to a frying pan.

Mom caught my eye and I raised my brows at her. She looked away and started telling a story about selling one of her rocks to Taylor Swift.

CHAPTER 24

· · · · · · · · · · · · · ·

Rule: *Always trust your first instincts.*

I held up one hand against a light shining in my eyes. "What's happening?" I whispered, groggy from sleep. I wasn't sure what had woken me—a noise, the light, a sense of impending doom.

My sister was still asleep in the other bed, only feet from mine.

"Nothing, sweetie. Go back to sleep." Mom collected something off the table behind me and then headed for the door.

"Where are you going?"

"I left a note. I'll see you tomorrow night."

"Tomorrow night?" My sleep-addled brain couldn't process that for a moment and by the time I did she was already out the front door. I threw the blanket off my legs, jumped up, and chased after her. She was already at her car. Crickets chirped, and there was a buzzing from an electric wire overhead.

"Mom, wait."

She turned, the backpack she wore shifting with her.

"You're leaving? Tomorrow is the Fourth." I walked down the stairs to join her so we didn't wake the whole commune.

"I left some instructions on how to get to the fireworks show. And I should be home by the time it's over."

"Where are you going?"

"A friend is doing this exploration hike that I've wanted to do forever. I'll be collecting rocks for my shop. Maybe some crystals if I'm lucky."

"An exploration hike?" I sighed out the disappointment I thought I'd let go of years ago. "Zoey came here to see you. Don't do this."

"It's not a big deal, Bird. I'll be gone less than twenty-four hours."

I crossed my arms and backed away. "Remember this moment, because this is the one you're going to lose her."

She laughed that annoying chirpy laugh of hers. "You're so dramatic, honey. Are you a teenager or a forty-year-old?"

"Which are you?"

"I'm not boring, that's what I am," she said with another laugh. "You learned this from your father."

"Being a responsible parent isn't boring."

"You and your guilt trips. Even at ten you were good at them. I can't handle your judgmental nature. It's twenty-four hours. Grow up." With that, she got in the car and drove away into the night.

I stared after her, sure I was supposed to feel something—betrayal, hurt, anger. But really, all I felt was numb. Until I thought of Zoey. She was not numb. Far from it. This would hurt her, and that made me sad.

I tossed and turned the rest of the night, not wanting to wake Zoey but unable to sleep. The second the rising sun turned the windows gray, I got out of bed, shrugged on a hoodie, and went outside. Maybe I was hoping it was all a dream. Or that I'd see my mom's car out there, proving that she'd changed her mind. It wasn't.

A mist hung in the trees as I walked, and dewy moisture clung to every green surface around me. My phone said it was six-fifteen. Too early to call anyone. A thought crept into my brain. Maybe a way to save today for my sister.

Is your cousin still taking you to a fourth of July party? What time and where?

I was surprised when Chad texted back almost immediately. *Yes*

Can my sister come too?

Of course. Do you want me to pick you up?

No, we have a car

Cool. I'll text you the address. It starts at four. Swimming and BBQ

You're up early, I responded.

So are you

Yeah, well, my mom had walked out on me for the second time. "How's that for drama, Mom?" I muttered under my breath.

See you later, I texted.

I took a lap around the compound and by the time I got back to the bus it was around seven and Zoey was awake. Reading Mom's note.

"She left?"

How was I going to play this off? I really wanted my sister to join me on this side of never trusting Mom again, but I also knew she had to cross that line on her own. She had to see it. I couldn't force her to.

"Just until tonight," I said, trying to sound like it was no big deal. I nodded toward the note. I hadn't read it, but assumed she'd written that.

Zoey's brows came together in concern as she read the note again. "Did she tell you about this?"

"I woke up last night when she was leaving."

"She left last night? Why didn't you wake me?"

"Because it was fast. And she'll be back tonight."

My sister nodded, trying to process, like I had. She had more goodwill toward our mom, which was probably why she said, "Yeah, yesterday out in the garden she was saying she was running out of supplies. I guess her business is doing well."

My eyes went to the rows and rows of rocks and crystals that lined the shelf above the windows. "Yeah, running out. I'm glad she's selling so many."

"So, fireworks tonight?" Zoey turned the piece of paper toward me.

"Did you ever meet Chad? One of my coworkers at the shelter?"

"Hot Chad?"

"Yes."

"I met him at that adoption thing at the park."

"Right. Well, he's here this weekend and his cousin is taking him to a party. He invited us."

I wasn't sure if Zoey was putting on a brave face for me, but her eyes drifted back down to the note and she emitted a heavy breath. "Sounds good."

Zoey had declared sometime later that morning she was going for a drive and left the bus without asking if I wanted to come. I assumed she needed some alone time to process. I understood. But now, several hours later, I was bored out of my mind. Asher was at the shelter—apparently the *Are you the chosen one?* post yesterday had caused an increase in traffic. Dogs were getting adopted. Unfortunately, not Bean. Yet.

A television was mounted on the metal wall between two windows. So far, Zoey and I hadn't turned it on. I did now, but the only thing that came on-screen was the DVD player connection indicating there was no disk. Apparently, our mom didn't have any streaming services. A cabinet sat below the television and I opened the door to find rows of movies. On the very end were smaller cases, containing what looked like miniature DVDs. It took me a minute to realize they were home movies with dates or words written across the front. I found one labeled *Wedding* and put it in the tray of the player.

The remote was on top of the cabinet and I turned up the volume and pressed Play. I'd seen pictures of my dad from when he was younger, but I'd never watched a video of him, and as I sat there cross-legged on my mom's couch in a bus watching their wedding ceremony and the reception, there was something about seeing my dad in motion that a photo could never capture. He had long wavy hair and an infectious smile. He danced and laughed loud and drank and wasn't weighed down with life.

An ache rose in my chest and leaked out my eyes. I swiped at my cheeks.

I watched the entire two-hour video and by the time I was done my face felt cold and clammy. I uncrossed my legs and stretched them out in front of me, my feet numb at first and then pins and needles. I stood and ejected the disk, then popped it back into its little square case. I started to put it back in the cabinet but stopped. Instead, I unzipped my suitcase and dropped it inside. I'd never stolen anything in my life, but this didn't feel like stealing. This didn't belong here.

I sighed and looked at my phone. It was nearing four. Where was Zoey?

Are you going to be home by four? I texted.

She didn't answer. Maybe she was driving.

Taking something from somebody that you don't think they deserve to have . . . good or bad? That text I sent to Asher.

He didn't answer right away either. I wished I hadn't come here. Or at the very least I wished Asher had. I needed him. I just wanted to wrap him around me and forget this ache in my chest. It was weird to need someone like this. I'd never let someone in enough to need them.

I went to the tiny bathroom to get ready and stared into the mirror. After just watching the twenty-year-old version of my mom on TV for the last two hours, my own image in the mirror brought a flare of anger. Why did I have to look so much like her?

I washed my face and put on some makeup, then went back to the living room and peered out the windows. This time I tried to *call* my sister. No answer. Maybe I shouldn't have let her go. She wasn't in a good headspace. What if she got in an accident or her phone battery died and she got lost? She wouldn't have driven all the way home. Or would she?

Anxiety was building up in my chest as I paced what would be an aisle if this were an operating bus.

At four forty-five, gravel popped under tires as Zoey pulled up. Relief poured down my spine. She walked inside like it was nothing and said, "You ready?"

"Are you?" I asked. We didn't have to go. "Are you okay?"

"Fine. Let's go."

CHAPTER 25

· · · · · · · · · · · · · · ·

Rule: No, seriously, always trust your first instinct.

"Chad!" I called when I finally saw him in the crowd of people in the backyard. We'd arrived about ten minutes ago and I felt like an imposter even though there were lots of people and nobody seemed to be paying much attention to us.

"I forgot how cute he was," Zoey said, swiping a bottle of beer as we passed a red tub full of ice and drinks. She was only twenty, but apparently that wasn't stopping her. My age was definitely stopping me at a stranger's house in a place I didn't know with our mother as the parent who'd have to save me from trouble.

"He's too young for you," I told my sister.

"Really? He's underage?"

"Yes, and so are you," I reminded her as she took a sip of beer. My sister wasn't a drinker. Or at least, as far as I knew she wasn't. I didn't think today, with how she must be feeling, was a good time to start.

"Ugh, do you always have to do that?"

"Do what?"

"Be so judgmental about everything?"

I flinched. Our mom had said pretty much the same thing last night, but coming from my sister, who rarely said a critical word, it hurt. "Sorry, I wasn't trying to." Because I really wasn't.

Chad must've heard my call because he weaved through the crowd, making his way to us. "Hey," he said with a smile. "Glad you found it."

"The internet makes it nearly impossible not to," I said.

My sister blew air between her lips.

Was that the wrong thing to say too?

Chad and I both looked at her and she held her hands up as though that had been an accident. She'd already finished half her beer.

A guy with long curly hair and a large nose sidled up to Chad. "Hey, cousin. Friends of yours?"

"Oh yes," Chad said. "This is Wren and her sister. And this is my cousin David."

"He is obviously not well practiced at introducing girls to people," David said.

"It's okay," I said. "He's not trying to impress me."

"Actually, I think I am."

I laughed, like it was a joke. It was a joke, right? Wait, Chad didn't tell jokes.

David looked at me, his eyes lingering a bit too long, then finally said, "You look so familiar."

"I don't live here, so I doubt it."

"Huh." He narrowed his eyes. "Do people say that to you a lot? Maybe you look like someone famous."

"No, they don't. Sorry." The only time guys had ever said that to me was when they were trying to pick me up or were trying to fill awkward silence. I hoped the former was not what was happening here.

"Weird," he said with a shrug. "And there's Christopher. See you later."

"Do you guys want something to eat?" Chad asked. "There's hamburgers and chicken, I think."

I glanced at my sister, who had just finished her beer. "Do you want food?"

"What did you say to her yesterday?" she asked.

"What?" I asked. "Who?"

"Mom. Did you two fight?" She'd obviously been thinking about it all day.

"No, we didn't. I was being nice."

She narrowed her eyes.

"Let's get food," I said.

"I'm going to find something to drink," Zoey said, and she left me there with Chad. I watched her go, my hope that this party would cheer her up gone.

"What was that about?" Chad asked.

Despite how open I'd been with Asher lately, I was still a very private person with most. "Mommy issues," I joked, trying to shake off Zoey's questions. I knew she was struggling with what our mom had done and I completely understood. I tried not to take it personally. "Point me to the barbecue."

My phone buzzed in my pocket. I pulled it out. It was a text from Asher that read: *Good?*

Not really, I texted back.

So you put it back?

What? Oh! I'd sent him that text about stealing my mom's wedding DVD.

"Asher?" Chad asked as we walked.

"Yeah, sorry." I was being rude. I sent a quick, *No. Talk later?* to Asher and tucked my phone away.

We passed a pool where some people were swimming, but most were just sitting with their feet in the water and sipping on drinks.

"Oh hey!" someone said as we passed. "It's you."

"Who's that?" I asked.

Chad shook his head. "I'm not sure. Maybe I met them last summer or something."

"Chad, too hot to remember people," I teased.

"You think I'm hot?"

I laughed. "Don't pretend you don't know that." It was so much easier to talk to someone once you weren't interested in them anymore.

"I mean, I thought I did. And then . . ."

"Bam. I have a boyfriend?"

"Exactly," he said.

"You were taking too long."

He chuckled. "I'll have to remember that next time."

"Seriously, if you want something, go for it."

His hand brushed mine.

I increased the distance between us. "I mean *next* time you want something."

"Right," he said.

We reached the food table and I picked up a plate. I surveyed the spread—fruit, chips, veggies, potato salad, and a big platter of barbecued meat. I hadn't eaten all day, but I wasn't feeling especially hungry. I filled up my plate anyway alongside Chad.

When we reached the end of the table I looked around for my sister. I didn't see her. Chad led me to a blanket that was spread out on the grass. A few other people were already sitting there, but it was a big blanket. We sat down.

"What have you been doing so far this weekend?" I popped a square of watermelon in my mouth.

"We were on the lake yesterday, boating."

"Wren!" David came running toward us, then plopped stomach-first in front of us. "You totally know why I recognized you! You're good!"

"What?" I asked.

"What?" he mimicked, and then laughed.

I felt my cheeks growing red and I didn't even know why.

"What are you talking about?" Chad asked.

"She's that TikTok girl."

"TikTok girl?" I asked, looking at Chad, who seemed equally as confused.

"Yes, the catfish one," David said. "It was staged, right? That's the debate."

"What?" I asked, something in my stomach becoming heavy and tight.

"Oh yeah," one of the girls sitting on the blanket said. "You *are* her. I wondered where I'd seen you before."

"Someone fill me in here," I said. "You've seen me on TikTok?"

"You honestly haven't seen it?" the girl asked.

David playfully patted my shoulder, "No, come on, you must be the world's best actress. This is why you made the video seem so real, these skills."

The girl, not as convinced as David that I was faking, passed me her phone. A TikTok video was on the screen.

"Maybe you shouldn't watch it here," Chad said, and I became aware that everyone on the blanket and several people around us had gone still and were watching me. He was probably right.

The frozen image was a blurry face that I knew would become clear when I pushed Play. There would probably be sound too. Did I really want to watch this in front of a group of strangers and Chad? Darren made the decision for me when he reached over and pushed Play.

Dale's face came into focus. The words *Part 1* were at the bottom of the video. Staring into the camera, Dale said, "So here we are out in front of the meeting place. We know she's not showing. We think, since she refused to meet up every time he asked, refused to send pics, and wouldn't even do a video call, that she is a catfish."

"*You* think that," Asher said from off camera.

"She ghosted you like two days ago when you gave her a *we need to meet or this is over* speech, right?"

The camera panned over to Asher, who rolled his eyes. "Yes, she did. But I'm getting ready to play the sad sack."

Next there was a montage of text messages. Probably the messages Asher and this girl had exchanged.

"Poor Asher," Dale said. "But his loss is our gain, because you know what gets tons of views? Sad stories. We're about to see Asher excited to meet his online crush and get crushed."

"Are you really going to post this video?" Asher asked. "Spelling out the fact that we're putting on an act?"

"No, this is just for fun," Dale said. Then words came on the screen that I had to pause to read. They said: *We were not going to post this video, but the following event made it necessary in order to tell the full story. Like for Part 2.*

The video ended and started playing again from the beginning. The pit in my stomach grew. My eyes went to the view count. It had well over a hundred thousand. That wasn't too bad as far as views went.

"He already told me that he knew I wasn't her. That he knew he was probably getting catfished," I felt the need to say out loud. I had assumed Asher didn't know until *after* the café, but it made sense that both he and Dale would want to attempt a viral post about it.

"There's another video," the girl said.

"I'm in it," I suddenly realized. Of course I was; that was why she and David had recognized me.

The girl nodded slowly.

I clicked on the username. I couldn't tell from the bio whose account it was—it didn't have either Dale's or Asher's name. The handle was HaveItYourWay. That phrase seemed familiar, but I couldn't remember where I'd read or heard it before.

I scrolled down until I found part two and clicked on it.

The video went almost exactly how I remembered that afternoon going. Dale and Asher walked in to the café, Dale making fun of Asher. And then there was a shot of me, in the corner. A flashing arrow and the words *Wait for it* appeared above my head. I hadn't realized they knew I was sitting there the whole time. Apparently, I hadn't been as hidden by the plant as I thought.

The video cut to the table, where the mocking continued.

"You're being so mean," Asher said.

"Uh, hello, maintain character," Dale said.

"Oh please, I'm a master editor. I can edit anything out."

"Part three already up," a voice said as the video ended.

I sighed and scrolled to the next video. What I thought would be a video of the Formica tabletop, due to Dale's shock at my arrival, was actually an upshot of him. He waggled his eyebrows at the camera as if happy with this turn of events. The shot of me in the corner from part two flashed on-screen along with the words *Remember her? She apparently felt the need to save my pathetic friend.* Then I heard Asher's voice. "Gemma?"

The camera panned to me. "Hi," I said.

Asher slid out of the bench seat and hugged me. "I told you I'd hug you when I saw you." Speaking of pathetic, the look on my face was that of a hug-starved loser. Whether this was Asher's account or not, the editing was very familiar. It was definitely Asher's editing.

"This is bad," I said out loud.

"You don't have to watch any more," Chad said.

"Over three million people have already watched it, why not you?" Darren said.

"What?" I asked, my eyes shooting to the view count. He was right—part three of the saga had well over three million views. "He used me to go viral." My voice cracked.

"Just turn it off," Chad said.

My finger shifted to the comments button.

"Don't read the comments," Chad said. "Comments can be very bad."

I didn't listen, I clicked because I was obviously a fan of self-inflicted punishment. The top comment, with over ten thousand likes and hundreds of responses, was *Someone who lies that easily is either in on the scam or a total sociopath.*

That comment was about me. Ten thousand people agreed with that comment.

"He left that up?" I said, more to myself than anyone. If this *was* Asher's account, he could've deleted the comment. It wouldn't have been hard. He had replied, though. His response read: *No, she's just super nice! A save-the-day-type girl.*

I narrowed my eyes. I had told Asher he was a save-the-day-type guy at one point. He was definitely not a save-the-day-type guy. He was a save-himself type guy, it seemed. That meant this *was* his account, didn't it? Dale hadn't heard me use that phrase.

"You okay?" Chad asked.

My heart felt like it was beating in my throat. I could hardly breathe. Everyone had gone quiet, watching me. Humiliation crept across my cheeks, burning my skin.

"So was it staged?" David asked as if this was just one big joke. "I'm on Team Staged."

"As opposed to Team Sociopath?" I snapped.

I handed the girl her phone. I didn't even know her name and her phone had destroyed my life in less than five minutes. I couldn't be here anymore. Why had I watched the video? I searched for my sister and finally spotted her across the yard, I beelined toward her, Chad on my heels.

Zoey was sitting in a camping chair, drinking a beer and talking with a small group of people. When I arrived, I said, "Can we go?"

"Ah, here she is," Zoey said. "My sister."

Everyone in the circle looked at me.

"We were just talking about you and everyone agrees, you must've said something to Mom yesterday. You promised you'd be nice if you came. I didn't even want you to come. You can never keep your judgmental opinions to yourself."

I swallowed through the lump in my throat that seemed to be growing. "Can we just go, Zoey?"

"I don't want to go. I'm having fun. Have you heard of fun?" She held up her bottle. "You were overjoyed when we first got into town and you saw how Mom lived. I could practically hear the *I told you so* in how you were acting. I'm sure Mom saw through your fake happy act too."

"That's not true. I didn't want you to be disappointed. I was trying to make the best of it."

"Why do you have to make the best of anything? Mom is fine. What was it that you thought was so shameful? That she lives on a bus? That she sells rocks?"

"No, it was more the leaving thing," I said. My voice was thick with emotion and I hated that all these strangers were seeing me like this.

"You sure aren't giving her any reasons to stay," my sister said.

I whirled around and took off across the yard. When I got out front, though, I didn't know where to go. Zoey had driven and our dad was hours away.

"Wren," a voice said from behind me.

I turned to see Chad standing there. "Do you want a ride?" he asked.

"When are you going *home* home?"

"Tomorrow."

"Can I go with you?"

"I'm giving David a ride too. He's visiting for a few weeks. Does that change your mind?"

It probably should've as I pictured David saying, *I'm Team Staged,* but it didn't. "No."

"Then yes, for sure."

CHAPTER 26

· · · · · · · · · · · · · · · ·

Rule: A surprise is a warning in disguise.

It really sucked when the person I wanted to talk to about everything that had happened was also the person I was never going to
talk to again—Asher.

After Chad dropped me off at my mom's bus, telling me he'd
pick me up in the morning, I listened to the fireworks boom outside far into the night as I lay in bed, past feeling. To go along with
the soundtrack outside, a text from Asher came through with a
picture of fireworks shooting over the bay. *Facetime so we can watch
a few together?*

I didn't respond.

Instead, I texted Kamala. *You around? I need to talk.*

My phone almost immediately lit up with a FaceTime call
from her. I answered. Her face was in shadows. "Hey! Are you
surviving?" A loud crack sounded and her eyes lit up.

"Where are you?" I asked.

She panned her phone across a scene that looked very similar to the photo Asher had sent. Then, before I could react, Dale's face was on-screen, followed by Asher's.

"Hi!" Asher said, and I nearly cried. "I see how it is. Best friend over boyfriend?"

Kamala laughed, then she came back on-screen. "Always," she said. "So what's up? Mom drama?"

I nodded because it was all I could do to keep the tears in check.

"I'm sorry. You're coming home in two days, though, right?"

"Tomorrow," I said.

"Really? Is that new?" More fireworks popped, both on-screen and out my window.

I nodded again.

"She's coming home tomorrow!" Kamala yelled as if this was the best news.

"Tell her I have a surprise for her!" Asher said. "A big one!"

Kamala smiled in what I assumed was his direction, like they were all three the best of friends now.

"I'm going to go," I said.

"What?" Kamala screamed.

I waved and hung up. She didn't try to call back or text. Neither did I.

Zoey came home several hours later, obviously sobered up. She checked our mom's bedroom, which was still empty, and grumbled something like, "Figures."

"You awake?" she asked.

I closed my eyes, pretending to be asleep.

The next morning, our mom was still not home. I packed my bag and when Chad sent me a text, I headed for the door.

"Where are you going?" Zoey asked, standing in the kitchen waiting for her toast to pop.

"Chad's giving me a ride home. You can text Mom and tell her I'm gone and you can have the experience you wanted to have with her all along."

She sighed. "Wren, wait."

"Oh, and while you're at it, ask her again to come to your graduation. Really pin her down. See how she reacts to that." I let the door shut behind me before Zoey could finish whatever she was going to say.

When I got to Chad's idling car, I threw my backpack and suitcase into the back seat and climbed in after them. "Hey," I said, buckling up.

"Hi," Chad said. His eyes met mine in the rearview mirror. Maybe he was gauging my mood today. I wasn't sure what he saw, how easy I was to read, but he didn't say anything else.

David was in the passenger seat and he turned all the way around and said, "I got the playlist, you cool with that?"

"So cool," I said.

Chad backed down the gravel drive and then drove along the dirt road to exit the commune. I leaned back in the seat, closed my eyes, and let them talk the entire way home.

I knew my dad would be home when I arrived, and even though I'd had hours to think about it, I still had no idea what I was going to say. I wondered if Zoey had given him a heads-up. And if so, had she put all the blame on me? When I opened the door, though, he gave me a surprised look. Meaning no warning had happened.

"I thought you guys weren't coming home until tomorrow."

"It's just me. I caught a ride with a friend. Zoey will be home tomorrow . . . I think." Who knew—maybe she would extend her trip now that I was out of the way.

"You left Zoey in Tahoe?" Dad asked, obviously trying to process.

"She has a car."

"That she will now have to drive home alone?"

"She'll be fine."

In a rare show of taking sides, he said, "You couldn't have lasted one more day with your mom to help your sister? I'm disappointed in you."

I didn't want to cry. Not in front of my dad. Not at all, actually. I channeled my emotions into anger instead and adjusted my backpack as I headed for my room. "Get in line," I said over my shoulder, then shut the door behind me.

The next morning, I was woken by my buzzing phone. I ignored it the first time, but whoever it was called back. I thought Asher's name would be on my screen and I'd have to start blocking his number, but when I picked up my phone I saw it was Erin.

"Hello," I answered, my voice deep from sleep.

"Wren, hey, Chad called in sick today, can you come in?"

I wanted to tell her I was still out of town, but she should've already known that, so maybe Chad had mentioned I was home when he called in. That little punk. I did not feel like working today. Just as I thought that, though, I pictured Bean. I hadn't seen him in days and I was sure he was the only one who could lift my mood at this point. Plus, maybe he needed me too. He hadn't been at the shelter through a Fourth of July yet, which could be a scary time for a lot of dogs. I wondered how Bean had handled it. Something familiar today would be good for him, and me. "Is an hour soon enough?" I asked.

"Yes, that's perfect. Thank you, you're a lifesaver!"

Her declaration reminded me of that stupid *save the day* comment Asher had left up on TikTok. I cringed. "Not really, but I'll see you soon."

We hung up and I checked my phone for any other notifications that might have come while I slept. There were none. None from my sister or Asher or even Kamala. I swallowed hard and went to get ready.

My dad had already left for work and I was glad we didn't have to have an awkward exchange this morning. I kind of hated everyone right now and I didn't need to say anything I'd regret.

An hour later I pulled into the parking lot of Petsacular, looking forward to hanging out with Bean and getting my mind off things. I must've already been in some kind of zone because I didn't process anything in the parking lot and when I walked inside and saw Asher standing there with his cute goofy smile and his lanky frame and his floppy hair, my first instinct was to smile back.

But then every emotion I'd felt in the last forty-eight hours hit me at once and my smile fell. He rushed forward and hugged me, not seeming to notice that I didn't hug him back. Why had it not occurred to me that he might be here?

"I missed you and I'm so excited! I have a surprise for you," he said. "Come here." He took me by the hand, led me across the mostly empty lobby and through the swinging door to the kennels. Erin was there. She gave me a wink and a thumbs-up. Had Asher asked her to call me in today?

"What's going on?" I asked.

"You'll see," Asher said, stopping suddenly before we rounded the last row of kennels. He turned to face me, his smile still on his face. "Close your eyes."

"No."

"Come on, it will make it more fun."

"Asher, I don't want to do this. We need to talk."

"That sounds serious," he said in his fake-serious voice, but then his smile faltered. "Is everything okay?"

I pulled my hand out of his. "No, it's not."

Colorful streamers flew out from behind the wall, unfurling into long strips, followed by handfuls of confetti. The dogs, which had already been barking, redoubled their efforts. I could no longer hear Asher even though I could see he was talking. Realizing this, he leaned close to my ear, and said, "Sorry, they were supposed to wait until they saw us. We'll talk after, okay?" He raised his eyebrows in a question.

I nodded and we rounded the corner. Rodrigo and Erin stood by Bean's kennel holding the ends of streamer rolls and looking sheepish. The dogs finally quieted a bit and Erin yelled, "Congratulations!"

Had Asher announced our relationship to the shelter? Were they throwing us a party? That didn't make sense. "For what?" I asked.

"You did it! You both did it! Bean was adopted!"

My eyes shot to the kennel behind Erin and Rodrigo. It was empty, aside from a few pieces of confetti that had made it through the chain link and lay strewn across the cement. "He's gone?" I asked, my voice so soft that I knew they couldn't hear it.

"This weekend was crazy," Asher said. "The line was out the door. We asked for an Arthur and we got one."

"What?"

"You know, your post? The sword in the stone? Arthur was the one who pulled it out."

Erin approached me and patted my arm. "Seriously, good job, guys. We should team you two up for other placements. You're like the dynamic duo."

Rodrigo gave Asher a high five and then he and Erin walked away.

I shuffled forward and grabbed hold of the chain links, peering into the empty kennel, not quite believing Bean was gone. "Why didn't you tell me?"

"You were out of town. I thought it would be a fun surprise."

"I didn't get to say goodbye." I turned to face Asher, my eyes welling up with tears. "Nobody thought I'd want to say goodbye?"

He cursed under his breath. "I wasn't thinking. Of course you would."

The first tear was hot as it slid down my cheek. I wiped at it angrily with the back of my hand. But it didn't matter; more followed fast. Asher took a step forward, his arms extended as though he was going to pull me into a hug. I put up both hands, blocking him. "Don't touch me."

"Wren, we can go see him. I'll get the info. It was Maggie. Remember Maggie from the rec center pool, that sweet little girl who loved him? I'm sure the fam—"

"Stop talking. Please. Just." I couldn't do this anymore. "I saw the TikTok videos."

Asher's mouth fell open, but nothing came out.

"That's your account."

He swallowed. "Dale's . . . and mine."

"You edit the videos. Does that make you a total sociopath or just in on the scam?" I said, reciting the post's most-liked comment, the one nobody had had the decency to delete.

He flinched, but said nothing.

"You edited them, right?" I wanted so badly for him to deny it. For him to tell me this was all a big misunderstanding and explain it all away.

Instead, he nodded.

"We're done." I stepped around him and left.

CHAPTER 27

· · · · · · · · · · · · ·

Rule: Don't give a boy the power to blow you up.

I wasn't even sure how I got to Kamala's house. I'd never cried so much in my life. And crying made everything blurry and snotty and stupid. But I made it and she pulled me inside and onto her big bed and handed me one of her squishy stuffed animals that I'd always made fun of. I hugged it to my chest.

"Do you want to talk or just cry?" she asked.

"I don't know," I said.

"I'm sorry your mom is awful."

"No, this isn't about my mom. Bean is gone."

The bed shifted as Kamala sat down beside me and put a hand on my arm. "I thought you'd be happy about that."

"I didn't get to say goodbye."

"I'm so sorry. I know you loved him."

"I hate Asher so much."

"Whoa, what?" Kamala looked taken aback. "He was just try-ing to help. He thought it's what you wanted."

228

"No." I took out my phone and pulled up TikTok. When I found the video, I passed my phone over.

Kamala watched without comment, my sniffles providing background noise. After she scrolled through the series of videos, she looked up. "Tell me he told you he was posting these."

"He didn't. You hadn't seen them?"

"No! I would've told you." She gasped. "This is what Becky and Meredith were talking about that day they came into the café. They had seen *this,* not the Bean Games footage."

I closed my eyes. "I'm so embarrassed for letting him use me like this. Did you see the comments?"

She clicked on them. After reading for a while, she said, "People are stupid."

"I don't care about people." The heat in my chest felt like it was going to set me on fire. "I cared about him." I took a hiccuping breath.

"I know. He's a jerk." Kamala picked up a yellow stuffed bird and twisted it between her hands. "Did he say why he did it?"

"Because he's a marketing overachiever who only cares about himself! He can probably use this in his portfolio."

"The catfish thing?" she asked.

"I was talking about the Bean thing, but yes! The catfish thing too. The editing genius."

"So it's his account?"

"Yes!" I exclaimed.

"And how did he explain himself? What was his excuse."

"I didn't let him explain. I left."

"I would've too. I'm sorry." Kamala hugged the bird to her

chest as if she needed comfort too. "Do you want me to call Dale and ask him about it?"

"No. You saw the videos. He was in on it too."

"That's true."

"The comments on the video, Kamala." I groaned. "Everyone thinks I'm a horrible person. Even my sister."

"Your sister?"

I filled her in on what had happened with my mom and what Zoey had said to me.

"Your sister has always defended your mom. I think it's her way of dealing with being left. You shut your mom out and she went the opposite way, pretended like it was fine, like it didn't hurt, overcompensated, tried to make excuses for her."

I nodded.

"But she shouldn't have acted like your mom taking off this weekend was your fault. You know it wasn't, right?"

"I know. I just want my sister to like me. I'm likable. Bean liked me." The tears came back full force.

Kamala lay down next to me and spooned me. "You have the biggest heart I know, Wren. I love you so much. I'm sorry that your sister was annoying and that Bean was adopted when you weren't there to say goodbye. And I'm sorry about Asher."

My shoulders shook with sobs and she held me tight.

The next day, after a restless night's sleep, nothing felt any better. My chest still hurt, my eyes stung, my throat felt raw. And it was all sinking in—what Asher had done, what Zoey had said, that Bean was gone. I needed to fix something and the only thing I had any control over at the moment was seeing Bean. So I got ready and drove to the shelter.

I knocked on the doorframe of the back office. Erin looked up from entering something into the computer.

"Well, hello there," she said.

I cringed, sure she'd heard about me fleeing the premises the day before. "Hi. I'm sorry I left work yesterday after you called me in."

"That's okay. I mainly called you in for the surprise."

"I was hoping that was the case."

"I heard you left because of a certain auburn-haired volunteer."

That was true, but I didn't want to bring Asher into this. "Sort of. It had more to do with Bean."

"Oh?" Erin tilted her head.

"I was sad that he was gone."

"Oh," she said, sympathy pulling down the corners of her mouth. "I'm sorry."

"I didn't expect to have that kind of reaction." I'd worked here for a year, and sure, I'd been sad when animals I had grown attached to left, but it was more a bittersweet sadness. This was different. This was just plain sadness.

"You were close with Bean. It's a perfectly reasonable reaction."

"I think I was hoping some miracle would happen and *I'd* get to adopt him." When Erin looked surprised by that statement, I added, "I know, I know, I didn't fill out any hold paperwork or put down a deposit. It was karma."

Erin laughed at my reference to the customer I'd pissed off at the beginning of summer. "I thought your dad was allergic to furred creatures."

"He is. It was never going to happen, but I guess in the back of my mind I still hoped."

"I understand. I've gotten pretty attached to some residents here myself."

"How do you get past it?"

"I take comfort knowing they're with their forever family and pour my love into another animal that needs it. There is no shortage of those. Like those kittens that were dropped off. They're doing well, but some kitten snuggles could help both you and them."

I was sure I could snuggle some kittens. I was sure I *would* do that. "It's just I didn't get any closure. I didn't get to say goodbye."

"That's hard."

I bit my lip and tapped on the doorframe. "Do you think . . . I mean, if I could just get the address of the family that adopted Bean so I could . . ."

Erin was shaking her head before I even finished. "I can't give you that, Wren. You know that. If you used an address for personal reasons, the whole shelter could suffer if the client chose to report us for that."

My throat tightened. "You think they'd report the shelter?"

"I have no idea, people are unpredictable and I can't risk that. I feel for you, I really do, but I can't give out personal client information."

I swallowed. "If he gets brought back for any reason . . ."

"You will be the first person I call."

I nodded for longer than I should've because it was the only thing keeping me from crying.

Erin straightened a stack of papers on her desk. "I'm not scheduling you with Asher anymore. Is that what you want?"

"Yes," I squeaked out. I jerked my thumb over my shoulder. "Can I work a little today? Clean out Bean's kennel?" I had noticed on my way in that it hadn't been cleaned yet. I could do that. Maybe it would give me a small amount of closure.

"You don't need to, Wren."

"I want to," I said, and then went to find a hose.

"Chad!" I called, jogging across the parking lot to catch up with him. The knees of my jeans were wet from where I'd been scrubbing the floor of Bean's kennel and my hands were red from being damp and cold for the last hour.

He turned and stopped to wait for me. "Hey."

"Are you sick?"

"Sick?"

"Didn't you call in yesterday?" I asked.

"No."

"Right." I'd forgotten Erin called me in for the surprise, not because Chad had called out. "Did I say thank you for giving me a ride home? I was out of it that day. I'm sorry I was bad company."

"It's okay. I would've been in shock too after seeing those videos. I kind of was."

"Yeah."

"I think . . . ," he started, then seemed to analyze his word choice, deciding on, ". . . we work together."

"What?" I was lost.

"I shouldn't have implied that I . . . I mean, we should be friends."

Oh. He was taking back his interest. Or he was telling me we were never going to get together. I held back the eye roll that I wanted to unleash on him. *Let him have this, Wren,* I told myself. It wasn't that I wanted to date Chad. But maybe I wanted him to still want to date me. It already felt like the entire world was breaking up with me right now.

"Yes, let's be friends," I said, determined, at least for the moment, not to feel sorry for myself.

"I . . . Are you okay?"

"Yes, of course. Thanks." Why was I thanking him?

"I heard about Bean. The unlovable dog has found a home. Congrats."

"He was lovable. He was very lovable." I pivoted toward my car, regretting stopping Chad at all.

"See you," he said.

I lifted my hand in a wave.

CHAPTER 28

· · · · · · · · · · · · ·

Rule: *Never date anyone who blames their*
mistakes on someone else.

For once in my life my dad wasn't predictable, because when I got
home, he was already there, two hours earlier than normal. And
sitting beside him on the couch was Zoey. They both looked at me
when I walked in.

I sighed. I didn't want to do this right now. My emotions were
already spent.

I started to walk by them, when our dad said, "Wren, please sit
with us. Zoey wants to apologize."

It wasn't until I sat down on the love seat across from them that
I noticed Zoey's eyes were red and shiny.

Dad looked expectantly at Zoey.

"Please don't say *I told you so*," Zoey said. Her voice cracked
with the words.

"Seriously?" I asked. "Why do you keep accusing me of that?
When's the last time I said it? When I was ten?"

"It's your eyes, Wren. They say it all the time."

"Is this an apology?" I asked. "Because it feels more like an attack." An undeserved one, in my opinion.

"I'm sorry, I'm sorry, you're right. I'm not doing a good job. I acted terribly at the party. I said things because I was hurt that Mom had left. I wanted to blame you so I didn't have to see how she really is."

"I wasn't *overjoyed* with how she was living," I said, using the word that Zoey had accused me with. "I saw you were surprised and upset and was trying to make you feel better."

"I know. I was terrible."

"When Mom came back did she tell you it wasn't me that made her leave? That I said nothing?"

"She didn't come back," Zoey said, softly.

I blinked. Even *I* hadn't predicted that. "She didn't come back?" Zoey shook her head no.

"That sucks," I said. "I'm sorry."

"Did it not bother you, too, when Mom left us in Tahoe?" she asked. "Why are you so calm about it?"

"Zoey, what you did and said hurt me way more than what Mom did this weekend. I had already put up boundaries with Mom. I didn't think I had to with you."

"But you *do* with me, Wren. You put them up with everyone."

"So do you. You just do it in a different way."

She looked at her hands in her lap. "You're right. And I don't want to. Not with you. I've been trying to ignore what Mom did for years and the comments you make about her, totally justified comments, always snap me back to reality. I think I just started resenting them and you for making them. I was shifting the blame. I've been a horrible sister."

My eyes began leaking again. Zoey stood and walked the ten steps between the couches and pulled me into a hug. "You're supposed to be my little sister," she said. "You're not supposed to have a better understanding of Mom than I do."

I gave a breathy laugh. "I'm just more jaded is all. You're soft and nice and you like everybody."

"You're soft on the inside even though you try to hide it. I've seen you with the animals. You have so much love to give. Don't let her close you up, Wren. Don't let anybody close you up."

Our dad joined us. "Can I get in on this?" He held his arms open and my sister and I stood and let ourselves be crushed in them.

"Thanks for being predictable and boring, Dad," I said.

"Um . . . you're welcome?"

"No, she's right," Zoey said. "We'd be screwed up without you. Mom was . . . is . . . so unreliable. Knowing I could always count on you helped me live."

I thought about the wedding video still sitting in my suitcase with the other things I hadn't unpacked yet. How free and fun our dad had been. After that, he became what he knew we needed and I loved him fiercely for that. I took a step back out of his arms. "But, Dad, we're basically grown now."

"You still have a few more years, but yes."

"If you want to take risks, try something you couldn't before because you had to carry everything on your back, we want you to. We're okay with a little uncertainty now. We want you to be happy." How had I not realized until this moment that my dad stayed at Niles's shop for us? It was the security we all needed.

"Yes, date! You should date," Zoey said.

"I was thinking opening your own shop, but sure, if you want to date, that's an option too," I said.

Our dad laughed. "I'm not sure I'll do either of those things right now, but that's sweet."

"But you could," I said. "We'll be okay, even if you crash and burn."

He nodded as what we were saying seemed to sink in. "It hasn't been a sacrifice, you know, raising you two. I've never felt burdened. It's been my pleasure."

My sister was crying again. Actually, so was I. And as we stood there, in a group hug, I knew that no matter how messed up the rest of my life seemed at the moment, everything would be okay. I had my family.

"On a level of one to ten, how ragey are you feeling right now?" Kamala said the next day as I sat in the corner of the coffee shop reading a book titled *Bird-Watching Your Way to Happiness*.

"Nine," I said.

"Nine? That high?"

"Well, I was a ten, but I've been reading about warblers and that took me down a point." I turned the book toward her, showing her a page full of colorful songbirds. "I wonder if my dad is allergic to birds."

"Think hard about those warblers because we're about to have a visitor."

"What? Who?" I turned toward the door. Dale was standing just outside it.

I closed the book with a loud smack and replaced it on the shelf. "Did you invite him here?"

"I'm just as surprised as you are."

Dale walked inside, the little bell announcing his entry like it was happy to see him. It was the only one. I narrowed my eyes at Kamala, who was wearing a small smile. Maybe the bell *wasn't* the only one.

"I was just leaving," I said, swiping my purse off the table and heading for the door.

"Please don't leave. Can we talk? I took the videos down," Dale said, as if that solved everything. "Even though they collectively had, like, ten million views."

"Excuse me for ruining your viral masterpiece."

"They kind of were. I don't get it."

I just wanted to crawl inside my shell and leave, but I wasn't willing to swallow my feelings this time. That hadn't served me well in the past. "You were making fun of me for the world to see and you expect me to what . . . be grateful that a ton of people saw you make fun of me? How do you not get that?"

"Making fun of you? How? When? We thought what you did was awesome. Funny, even. We weren't mocking you at all. We were immortalizing you. Praising you."

"*Immortalizing* me?" I asked, anger still burning in my chest. "If you thought what you were doing was so noble, Dale, you would've asked my permission."

He raised his hands in surrender. "Fair enough. But can we be real? If you weren't so surprised by your discovery of the video, if you were just watching it objectively, would you really be feeling all this? Wouldn't you think it was just a good, entertaining video?"

"But that's the point," Kamala chimed in. "She *was* surprised by it. She thought you were her friends, but what you did made it seem like you were using her for fame."

"I was hurt," I admitted, because I was.

Dale's eyes shot to the floor before they met mine. "That wasn't the intention. It really wasn't. Seriously, we never meant to hurt you. *Asher* would never want to hurt you. This dumb TikTok thing was all me. Be mad at me, not him."

"Don't worry, I'm mad at both of you."

"He's pretty torn up about this," Dale said. "Is there something else I can do? Do you want me to record a video telling everyone I'm an idiot? I will."

"As tempting as that sounds, no, I don't."

"What, then?" he asked. "What will help?"

"Nothing, Dale. Tell Asher it's over."

"I think you're making a mistake."

"Good thing I don't care what you think," I assured him.

He nodded, resigned, and left.

"Do you think Asher sent him?" I asked when Dale was gone.

"I don't know," Kamala replied.

"Why didn't he just come and face me himself?"

"You would want him to do that?"

"Better than trying to shift the blame to his friend." Is that what he was doing? He thought Dale could march in here and say it was all his fault and I'd be fine? "He knew I hated being online. I hardly put myself out there on my *own* page."

"True," Kamala said. "Do you think Dale is still going to make Asher humiliate himself at his party tomorrow night for getting catfished?"

"That's tomorrow night?"

Kamala nodded.

"If he does, Asher would probably be in on it. For the views."

Kamala hummed. "And that would prove that all he cares about, all they *both* care about, are TikTok views."

Were they going to stage some sort of public act of humiliation that they could post online? That thought made me angry. "We should go, then, right? Let them feel stupid doing their TikTok thing with us watching."

"We should definitely go," she agreed.

CHAPTER 29

• • • • • • • • • • • • •

Rule: *Abandon all rules. They can't save you in the end.*

"Did you seriously buy Dale a birthday present?" I asked Kamala as I picked up the wrapped box in the passenger seat and sat down.

"It felt weird going to his birthday party empty-handed."

"He's lucky I'm not giving him a punch in the face for his birthday."

She laughed a little.

I buckled my seat belt and shook the box. "What is it?"

She pulled out onto the road. "Um . . . just something I thought he needed."

"Oh, that clears it up."

"It's a GoPro."

My mouth fell open. "You bought Mr. Rich another way to record things?"

"I bought it before the TikTok thing. But now that you say it like that, yes, I should've just left it at home."

I groaned. "You like him, don't you?"

"Before . . . when he hadn't . . . I don't know!"

Why wouldn't she? Between the Bean Games and our catfish dates, Asher and I had thrown them together at every possible turn. "You can like him. He didn't do anything to you."

"After what he did to you? No way. That has to be on your list of dating rules, right? *Never date a guy who screwed over your bestie.*"

"My dating rules suck. They were a form of protection that didn't work in the end."

"What?" Kamala gasped in faux surprise.

"I know. That's what you've been telling me forever."

She reached over and grabbed my hand. "I always understood why you needed them."

As we neared our destination, the anger that had convinced me showing up at Dale's birthday party was the only reasonable thing to do was quickly wearing off. It was replaced with shallow breathing and nervous energy.

It must've been obvious because Kamala asked, "Are you going to talk to Asher tonight? Or are we strictly going to give them death glares while they record social media stunts?"

"I think the second option? I haven't decided yet." My body seemed to be shutting down, making the decision for me. I wanted to tell Kamala to turn the car around, that I'd changed my mind. I didn't want to see Asher. I was still hurting too much, regardless of how hard I was trying to ignore it.

There were so many cars at the house when we arrived—the entire circular drive was packed as was the street—that we had to park halfway down the block and walk. The sun had set and the sky was a chalky gray. The side gate was open, so we headed that way. Unlike the last time we'd been in Dale's backyard, it was full of people. People in the lit pool and in the pool house, people dancing on the grass to loud music. People eating and drinking on the large covered patio. A table stacked full with wrapped gifts was also on the patio. Kamala pointed her present toward it. I nodded and followed her.

"There are so many people here!" she yelled at me. "I don't even know this many people!"

"Dale probably doesn't either," I said.

Why were we here? Asher and Dale wouldn't care about us watching them try to go viral online . . . again. They wouldn't even know we were here. We reached the gift table and Kamala studied it like a game of Jenga, trying to figure out where she could put her box without knocking any of the others over.

"Are you wishing you hadn't bought him such an expensive birthday present now?" I asked, staring at his haul.

"Yeah, sort of," she said.

"It's not too late to take it back."

Kamala gave a nervous laugh and placed the box on top of a larger one. I wondered what her card said. Did it profess her undying love?

We both turned at the same time to head back into the yard when I nearly ran someone over. It was Elinor—Asher's ex.

"Sorry," she said, coming to a halt. Her eyes flitted over me, recognition coming onto her face. "It's you." She laughed. "I knew it was you on the beach, but Asher kept diverting."

"Me?" I asked, my brain trying to catch up to what she was saying.

"TikTok girl."

I didn't think the same bit of information could hurt me in a new way, but here I was being hurt all over again, realizing that yes, Asher was trying to divert on the beach, keep her from saying anything. "Right," I said. "It's me."

She shook her head. "Those guys are something else." Then she walked away, laughing to herself.

I kept my eyes on her.

"Was that—" Kamala started.

"Yes," I said, still watching Elinor work her way across the lit patio and then onto the grass. Halfway across the yard she stopped at a group and that's when I saw him. His tall lanky form, his floppy auburn hair. He was standing next to Dale and he looked over when Elinor arrived at his side. His expression was hard to see from this far away.

"We can leave," Kamala said, obviously watching Elinor as well.

"Do you think they're back together?" I asked, my voice catching a bit.

"No, I don't," she said. "He was literally talking about you nonstop less than a week ago when we were watching fireworks. Seriously, it was annoying."

Asher shook his head and crossed his arms, but from this distance I couldn't tell what they were saying.

The music stopped playing and some feedback rang through the speakers followed by silence.

"Hello, is this thing on?" Dale's voice echoed through the yard.

Kamala pointed to the deck by the pool. Dale was standing there, a microphone in one hand, his other arm extended to the side. "Hey, everyone! Welcome to my birthday party! Thanks for coming."

Some people shouted, but most had quieted down and were listening.

"In a few minutes we're going to be recording a series of videos, so if you all could clear this area around the pool for like thirty minutes, that'd be cool."

"Why'd you take the best ones down?" someone shouted, followed by a lot of other people echoing the sentiment. Tension spread through my chest.

I was so focused on Dale that I didn't see Asher walk across the yard, but suddenly he was right there, snatching the microphone from Dale's hand. "The real question should be, why did we put them up in the first place? Recording someone without their permission is what tools do. We were huge tools."

"I think you mean *are*!" a girl with rainbow hair shouted. "You *are* huge tools!"

A spattering of laughter sounded around the yard.

"I would agree with that," I muttered to Kamala.

"Get on with your videos! This is boring!" a person directly behind me yelled.

Before I could turn my head or hide my face, Asher's eyes, searching for the voice, collided with mine.

"You're here?" he said, almost like he didn't mean to say it out loud.

I took a step back.

"Please don't leave."

My heart jumped into my throat and my legs propelled me

backward. I did not want whatever public display was about to happen. I whirled around and darted through an open sliding glass door and into the house. I was doused with cold air the second I stepped inside.

The house was like nothing I'd ever seen in real life before. It was gorgeous with lots of shiny surfaces—floors and countertops and artwork. It also had more rooms than one family could possibly need. Especially since that family had only two kids.

I opened several doors in an attempt to find a place to hide, but every room looked too pristine to disturb. I ended up in what could only be Dale's room. Surprisingly, it had very little of Dale in it. It was as sterile as a hotel room. The only reason I knew it was his room was a pair of blue Vans by the closet door that I'd seen him wear before.

I sank onto the bed, not sure why this was where I'd chosen to flee. I should've left entirely. But when a knock sounded at the door and my heart stuttered, I knew that I hadn't wanted to leave. I knew I desperately wanted to talk to him.

"Wren," Asher said in a husky voice through the door. "Can I come in?"

I opened the door.

He stood in the hall looking . . . amazing. He looked amazing. His hair had just the right amount of body tonight and it fell perfectly across his forehead. His green T-shirt made his eyes pop and they looked bright and sad all at once.

My heart was beating in my ears, making it hard to hear. I opened the door wider and he came inside.

"I'm sorry," he said. "I'm so sorry."

My eyes stung with held-back tears. "I trusted you and I don't trust anybody."

His eyes were shiny too. "I know. There's really no excuse for it. I didn't know you back then, but I thought you were cool and fun and I wasn't thinking about what would happen to that video online. I seriously thought it would get twenty views like all our other videos. I hadn't been paying attention to it and didn't realize. Dale gets all the notifications. I just do the editing and . . . I'm sorry."

I pressed my knuckles below my nose, willing the tears to stay locked away. "And when Elinor almost told me about it on the beach? You didn't think about it then?" That's what had happened that day. She hadn't been confused because she was his catfish; she was confused because she'd seen me on TikTok.

"She follows Dale," Asher said. "I thought she was one of the twenty views we'd gotten. And I know her, she likes to stir things up. I just thought she was going to be mean about it. I should've told you. I have no good excuse. I just should've told you."

Why did my entire soul want to forgive him just like that? "And tonight? Clearing the pool area for a video? More attempts to go viral?"

"Sort of. But it was for you."

"For me?"

"I was going to record an apology to post online. I wanted people to understand that we're the bad guys, not you." Asher smiled a sad smile. "You were only trying to help me. It's honestly the nicest thing anyone has ever done for me."

"I want to believe you," I said.

"But you can't?" he asked.

"Why post an apology video during Dale's birthday party? It's loud and noisy and full of—"

"People," he said. "People who will share it with other people. I want every person who saw the first ones to see this one."

"Quite the marketing genius," I said.

"My parents would be proud," he returned in a low, sarcastic voice.

"If you think I need some huge viral apology, maybe you don't really know me. I thought you knew I didn't like all my business online. I think that"—I nodded toward the backyard—"was for you. To make *yourself* feel better."

He was quiet for a moment as if analyzing my statement. "What do *you* need?"

That was the question, wasn't it? I wished I knew. I wished I could say *Just hug me and it will all be better.* A few tears finally escaped. "I don't know," I answered honestly. "I guess I need time."

Asher lifted his glasses and swiped a palm across his right eye. "I can give you that."

CHAPTER 30

• • • • • • • • • • • • •

Zoey poked her head in my room. "Want to watch a movie?"

It had been a few days since the party, and maybe our dad had told her I needed cheering up. I had been extra mopey around the house.

"What movie?" I asked.

"Does it matter?" she answered.

"Yes, I do not want to watch anyone falling in love."

"Ah, I see. I can work with that. No love, only death."

I rolled off my bed and padded across the carpet to where she stood. She draped her arm around my neck. "I'm sorry about Olive Garden Boy."

"Me too," I said. For three days now I had been trying to decide what would make me feel better. What he or I could do or say that would fix everything. I still felt terrible, and I was sure he did as well. I didn't want to think about it anymore. I was scared I'd never figure it out. That nothing would actually work. I should've been okay with that, taken it as a sign that we weren't meant to be, but that didn't sit well with me either.

"Popcorn?" Zoey asked.

"I don't know if we have any."

"I thought you knew the contents of the pantry by heart. Don't you have it organized alphabetically?"

"No, I don't. It's organized logically."

"I have no idea what that means," she said.

I let out a breathy laugh. "I don't either."

While we were in the pantry rooting for popcorn, our dad appeared in the doorway. "Hey, Wren, there's someone at the front door for you." He had a rare full smile on his face.

Instantly every nerve in my body buzzed to life in anticipation. "There is?"

He nodded.

"I found the popcorn!" Zoey said, holding up a plastic-wrapped package.

"How do I look?" I ran my fingers through my hair. I had never gotten ready today and it was six o'clock at night. I still had on a pair of blue pajama pants, in fact.

"You look gorgeous," Zoey said.

I rushed out of the kitchen and through the living room. The front door was closed. Dad hadn't let Asher in?

I swung the door open, not willing to take the time to sort out the details of why my dad left him on the porch. But instead of Asher, a little girl stood there. Now I was even more confused. She smiled up at me, and recognition slowly worked its way into my mind.

"Maggie?" I asked.

She nodded.

I gasped, realizing what this meant. It took everything in me not to rush around her in search of Bean. "Is he here?"

She giggled and reached for my hand. I provided it without question. She led me down the path to where Bean stood with Maggie's mom on the sidewalk.

"Hey, boy!" I called.

Maggie's mom let go of the leash and Bean came barreling toward me, knocking me onto the grass and proceeding to lick my face and wag his tail at the same time.

"I missed you, too," I said.

He moved from me to Maggie, who sat right next to me on the grass. He licked her face and then mine again. He repeated this several times until Maggie and I were both laughing.

"Okay, Bean," I said. "Sit down. Let me look at you."

It took him another five minutes to do that. When he finally did, Maggie's mom joined us on the grass.

"Thank you for bringing him," I said. "I never got to say good-bye." Tears were welling up in my eyes.

"Asher told us," Maggie said.

"Asher . . . how?"

"He found us on Instagram," Maggie's mom said. "I'm Courtney, by the way."

"I'm Wren. Thank you so much. This is the best day ever. How is Bean doing?"

"We love him," Maggie said.

"We really do," Courtney agreed. "He's a character."

"He is." I scratched Bean behind the ears. "You have a home now. Are you so happy?"

As if he understood me, he gave a playful bark. I hugged him around the neck.

"Does this make it harder or easier?" Courtney asked, seeming to think I was going to scoop Bean up and steal him away from them. Part of me wanted to do just that. But a bigger part of me knew he was in the right place and that's what I had needed to see.

"It makes it better," I said.

Bean laid his head on my lap.

"If you guys ever go out of town and need a dog sitter, or if he just wants a playdate some afternoon . . ."

"We will absolutely call you," Courtney said. "Can I get your info?"

"Yes, please." We exchanged numbers and sat and visited for a while longer. "Thanks for coming. You really didn't have to do that," I said.

"That Asher makes a compelling argument. He's a sweetheart," Courtney said as she stood up and brushed grass off the back of her jeans.

"He is . . . ," I said.

"He promised to help me make a video," Maggie said.

"For TikTok?" I asked.

"No, my mom doesn't let me have TikTok. I want to make a funny video with Bean for my family's Instagram."

"He's good at those," I said.

"Bean or Asher?" Courtney said.

"Well, both, but I meant Asher," I replied.

She pulled a folded piece of paper out of her pocket. "This is for you."

"Bye, Wren," Maggie said. Bean jumped to his feet and was at her side. She gathered his leash and cooed some sweet words to him.

"Bye, Maggie. I can tell he loves you."

She beamed.

"Bye, Bean," I said, and he seemed to smile at me over his shoulder. I waved goodbye as they climbed in their car and drove away.

I waited until they were all the way around the corner before I opened the note. *I do know you,* it read. *I hope this helps you feel a little better.*

I smiled big. Asher was right. This was what I had needed. Not just to see Bean, although that was amazing, but for Asher to show me that he saw me.

I went into the house and plopped next to my sister on the couch. She extended the bowl of popcorn in my direction. "You thought it was Asher, didn't you?"

"You *do* know his name."

"I do. And did you? Think it was him?"

I took a handful. "Only because I never would've guessed Bean."

"Were you slightly disappointed it wasn't Asher, though?"

"No, I'm so happy I got to see my dog."

"Okay, fine. would you have been even happier if it had been Asher holding Bean's leash?"

"Why are you Team Asher all of a sudden?"

"Because of the look on your face in the pantry when you thought it was him."

I shoved Zoey's shoulder.

"Go see him," she said.

"But our movie."

"This will be better."

CHAPTER 31

. . . .

I knocked on the door and willed my heart to calm itself. It wasn't that I thought Asher wouldn't want to see me, but I did wonder if things would feel the same or if everything would be different, cracked.

The door swung open to reveal Mrs. Linden. "Oh, Wren," she said, her hands flying to her mouth in surprise and delight. "I am so happy to see you. I heard what Asher did and I've never been more disappointed."

"Does he tell you everything?" I asked, amused.

"I sure hope not." She smiled at me.

I handed her the gift I'd bought her several weeks ago. "Sorry for sitting on your couches. I hope these help."

She laughed. "You're a sweetheart. Asher's in his room. He might be napping. He woke up pretty early this morning trying to arrange something with a dog?" She shrugged. "I don't know."

"I do." I took several steps toward the hall, then said, "Does he wake up from a nap pleasant or grumpy?"

"He's a joy, Wren. But I'm his mom, so I'm a bit biased."

"He *is* a joy," I said. "But I might be biased too."

I let myself in Asher's dark bedroom and stood there, letting my eyes adjust. He had the ceiling fan on and was buried beneath several comforters, a tuft of auburn hair the only part of him that was visible.

I climbed on the bed next to him and peeled back the top comforter to see he was facing the wall, away from me. I listened to him breathe for a moment, watched his shoulders rise and fall, savored the last moment before whatever was going to happen happened. Then I reached out my hand and ran it down his blanket-covered back.

He took a deep breath and rolled onto his stomach. "What time is it?" he said in a scratchy voice.

"Like six-thirty or so," I said.

He went very, very still. He didn't even seem to be breathing for a full minute. Finally, he rolled toward me and opened his eyes. He stared at me for a while longer before he said, "Am I dreaming?"

I smiled at his adorable sleep-face, complete with puffy eyes and a blanket-pattern-imprinted cheek. "It depends. Would this be a good dream or a bad dream?"

"It would be the best dream."

"In that case, no, you are not."

He pressed his palms against his closed eyes, then dragged his hands down his face and focused on me again. "My mom keeps letting you in my room when I'm less than suitable for company."

"She seems to like me," I said. "But I have a feeling she likes everyone."

"Surprisingly, she doesn't, so you should feel special."

"I do," I said.

He sat up and for the first time I realized he was shirtless.

"Do you watch all your ex-boyfriends nap?" he asked, reaching over to his nightstand for his glasses.

My throat tightened with his use of the word *ex*. I didn't like that word in reference to him. "No, you should feel special."

"I do." He looked down at his chest. "Can I just . . . ?" Then he cupped his hand over his mouth and let out a breath. "And, yeah, I'll be right back."

"Please, take your time. I haven't seen you in a while, but do what you must."

He smiled, hopped out of bed, grabbed a T-shirt from his dresser, and then ran to the bathroom, I assumed to brush his teeth.

I sat there, suddenly nervous again. My stomach was in knots. It was so good to see him, but so far it *was* different. We were being careful and my wall was still very much in place even though I'd hoped it would immediately come crashing down when I saw Asher. And he seemed to have a wall up that he'd never had before.

When he came back, fully clothed, he flipped on the light and sat on the end of his bed. "You're here," he said with his signature smile.

I nodded and swallowed. "I'm here."

Why was he making me put my wall down first? Why hadn't he

hugged me yet? I needed his hug to know this was all going to be fine. That he still wanted us to be fine. "I brought you a present."

"You brought me a present?"

"Remember, the one I bought in Tahoe. It's nothing earth-shattering," I said, suddenly self-conscious.

He held out his hands.

I pulled out the red cape from my purse. It had a big blue *S* on it. Asher's eyes, which had been lit in anticipation, seemed to dim a little. "A cape . . . thank you."

"You hate it," I said.

"Are you mocking me? Because I always have to save the day? Because I was trying to help Dale go viral and ended up hurting you?"

"What? No! No, no, that's not it. It's not a joke gift. I really do think of you as a save-the-day type of guy and I love that about you. I'm sorry. It's a bad gift. I got you this too." I set the cape on his dresser and rooted around in my purse for the Twix I'd brought, his favorite candy.

When I turned around to give it to him, he was standing in front of me. Close.

"It's a great gift, Wren. Thank you. I just wasn't sure if you had forgiven me. I wasn't sure if you were here for closure or because . . ."

"Because what?" I asked when he didn't finish.

"Or because you wanted . . . me."

I nodded. I could let my wall down first. It had been up my whole life, after all, and he'd already helped me destroy it once. It was time to do it myself. "I do. I want you."

He raised one side of his mouth in a half smile.

"Do you want me?" I asked.

"I brushed my teeth, Wren. I saw you and I brushed my teeth."

"Is there something significant about brushing your teeth?" I asked, feigning innocence. "Most people do that every day. Twice a day, even. They—"

He pulled me against him into the tightest, best hug he had ever given me. I hugged him right back, holding on to him with everything in me. "I missed you so much," he said, burying his head into the space where my shoulder met my neck.

I threaded my fingers into his hair. "I missed you too. Thank you for bringing me Bean today. Thank you for knowing that would help."

"I was trying to make it up to you, Wren. I was just trying to make it better." His voice was scratchy again.

"You did. You did."

"I'm sorry I didn't wait for you to say goodbye in the first place."

"No, I'm happy he found a home."

"Me too."

"Now, I'm tired of waiting. Put that freshly brushed mouth on mine," I said.

He laughed, and when his laughter trailed off, he said, mouth against my neck, "I'm so sorry about the video. I'm sorry I hurt you."

"It's okay, I know you didn't mean to."

He pulled me to him, smashing his lips against mine. I answered just as intensely. He stumbled backward, taking me with him, until we were falling onto his bed. Our legs wrapped around each other's, our hearts in sync, and every last wall crumbled to the ground. "I love you," I said against his mouth.

He pulled back to look at me, our limbs still tangled together. "I was supposed to say that first."

"I love you," I said again. "Now you can only say it for the third time. How embarrassing for you."

He gasped and then tickled my sides.

I squealed and rolled onto my back to escape. He rolled as well, the upper half of his body hovering over me. He kissed me, slow and deep. "I love you, Wren."

CHAPTER 32

. . . .

Rule: *Dogs > People.*

"Do you think he'll like everyone now?" Asher asked as we drove to the park to meet up with our friends. Bean was on his lap, his head out the window. His tail hadn't stopped wagging since we'd picked him up for a playdate.

"Do I think he turned into a different dog in the last month? No." I said, flipping on the blinker and turning right, into the parking lot.

"You said the shelter stresses dogs out. Maybe Bean minus stress is an angel."

I laughed. "Are you an angel now, Bean?"

He gave a happy bark.

"He said no." I pulled into a parking space and turned off the car.

In the distance, sitting on a blanket under a tree, were Kamala, Dale, and Brett.

"Do you think Kami and Dale . . . ?"

"What?" Asher asked. "Do I think they secretly kiss?"

I laughed. "Do you?"

"Is that what you were going to ask?"

"I mean, basically."

He opened his door and let Bean out, holding on to his leash. "Maybe. I've been trying to figure that out."

Kamala had basically confessed that she liked Dale on the way to his party over a month ago, but she'd deflected all my questions about it since. "Me too."

"Would it bother you?" Asher asked.

"I don't think so." I opened my door and stepped out.

"Me neither," he said, throwing me a smile over the top of the car.

"You're late," Kamala said when we arrived at the blanket.

"Sorry, we had to pick up Bean."

"Hey, Beano," Kamala said.

Bean took one look at Kamala and immediately started walking back toward the car.

She shook her head. "So it wasn't lack of sleep like you claimed. I'm offended."

I shrugged. "I mean, sleep can only do so much for a personality."

"A universal truth," Asher said.

I sat and patted the blanket next to me for Bean to sit down. He gave a good hard look at the others sitting there before deciding that he could lie down between me and Asher.

"See, he's still a punk," I said to Asher.

"What does it mean that he likes us?" Asher asked.

"It means you're both punks," Kamala said. "Big ones."

"So true," Brett said. "Who brought the food to this thing?"

"We brought the dog," I said. "I thought someone else was bringing the food."

"Ugh," Brett groaned. "So lame. In fifteen minutes, someone is going on a food run."

"I'll go," Kamala said.

"Me too," Dale said.

Asher and I exchanged a look.

"What?" she asked.

"Nothing." I patted Bean's back. "I think we should reinstate the Bean Games."

"He's been adopted," Dale said.

"Did they return him?" Kamala asked, wide-eyed.

"No, no. I mean for some of the other animals in the shelter. The ones who are having a harder time being placed."

"But the games didn't really work for Bean," Kamala said.

"That's because he didn't have the right personality for them. But I think some of the other dogs do."

"I like this idea," Asher said.

"I like you," I said.

"I like you back."

"Stop!" Kamala said.

"Good thing you were so mean that first day, Dale," Asher said, "or she wouldn't have felt sorry for me."

"I call the next fake-catfish scenario!" Dale said.

"I do not recommend the lying part," I said. "Or the posting-without-permission part."

"So," Dale said, "are you giving me permission to repost?"

Everyone groaned.

"For the views!" he said. "Ten million views!"

Bean let out a bark.

"I'm going to take him on the playground," Asher said, hopping to his feet.

I stood too. "Sounds fun."

Asher grabbed my hand as we walked toward the slide. "Do you think I would have stood a chance with you if this dog hadn't liked me?"

I started to say, *Of course you would've,* but then I remembered that first day at the shelter, walking down the hall, seeing him holding the end of Bean's leash. It was the first time I had really looked at him, had really wanted to look at him. "Probably not."

He laughed. "That's what I thought. Thank goodness this dog likes punks."

I pulled his hand toward me, bringing him closer, then pushed up on my tiptoes and kissed him.

ACKNOWLEDGMENTS

Little did I know that after finishing the first edit of this book, we would lose our sweet rescue dog, Harley. He was with us for almost ten years. We adopted him from our local shelter when he was three. He was the very best dog—a Great Dane/Lab mix. A gentle giant at over one hundred pounds. He was the sweetest dog in the world and we miss him so much. If you're considering becoming an animal parent, I hope you will check out your local shelters. They are full of deserving animals waiting to share their love, like Bean and his friends.

Thank you, readers, for making this, and all my books, possible. Without you, I wouldn't get to keep writing. Thanks for the love and support of my books!

Michelle Wolfson, you are amazing! Sixteen books and counting together. I'm so happy I chose you as my agent. It makes my job easier to have you backing me up. Thanks for loving my books and being so awesome at your job.

Thanks to my editor, Wendy Loggia, for pushing me to make this book just right. You really made it so much stronger. I'm lucky to have you. And to Wendy's assistant, Ali Romig, for keeping me on track and providing great insights. Thanks to my publicist, Lili

Feinberg, for never getting tired of having to remind me of things. And thanks to the whole team at Delacorte: editor Hannah Hill, who gave great insight on this story, copyeditor Heather Lockwood Hughes, interior designer Cathy Bobak, associate director of copyediting Colleen Fellingham, production manager Brennam Bond, SVP and publisher Beverly Horowitz, president and publisher Barbara Marcus, and managing editor Tamar Schwartz. And the cover! Isn't it amazing? Thanks to the cover designer, Ray Shappell, and the cover artist, Charley Clements, for their beautiful work.

As always, thanks to my wonderful cheerleader of a husband, Jared; my kids, Skyler, Autumn, Abby, and Donavan; and my son-in-law, Joe. I'm so lucky to have you all in my life. Thanks for always being supportive and encouraging. You all make me so proud to be your mom.

I have so many wonderful friends who help me in different aspects inside and outside of writing. Thank you to Stephanie Ryan (who is also my very talented bio photographer sister), Brittney Swift, Emily Freeman, Mandy Hillman, Megan Grant, Candice Kennington, Renee Collins, Jenn Johansson, Bree Despain, Shannon Messenger, Natalie Whipple, Michelle Argyle, Debra Driza, Amy Tintera, Elizabeth Minnick, Misti Hamel, and Claudia Wadsworth.

Last, but never least, thanks to my big, fun, amazing family: My mom, Chris DeWoody, and her husband, Mark Thompson. My dad, Donald DeWoody, who passed in 2006 and who I think about and miss often. My brothers and sisters, Heather and Dave Garza, Jared and Rachel DeWoody, Spencer and Zita DeWoody, and Stephanie and Kevin Ryan. My husband's parents, siblings, and spouses—Vance and Karen West, Eric and Michelle West, Sharlynn West, Brian and Rachel Braithwaite, Jim and Angie Stettler, Rick and Emily Hill. I also have thirty nieces and nephews. Plus great-nieces and great-nephews! And I love all of these people with all my heart. I feel so lucky to have such a big, close family.

Stay tuned for more books coming your way. And please reach out to me on social media. I love connecting with readers! Thank you again for reading my books!

KASIE WEST
AUTHOR OF *SUNKISSED*

PLACES
WE'VE
NEVER
BEEN

A family RV trip across the country puts
Norah on an unexpected road to romance!

TURN THE PAGE TO READ AN EXCERPT

"NORAH, BREATHE," WILLOW SAID WITH A LAUGH. "I swear I've never seen you this excited in my life. I'm starting to get jealous."

I swatted her arm with a folded blue sweatshirt, then added it to the open suitcase on my bed. "You *should* be jealous," I teased. "He was my best friend for most of my life. You only just passed three years."

"I think *was* is the key word there."

She was right, of course. I hadn't seen Skyler since the summer before eighth grade. That's when he and his family moved across the country to Ohio. We'd Snapped and messaged and texted a lot that first year, but every year since, we'd drifted more and more apart until we basically had zero communication. Now all we did was occasionally like each other's posts on Instagram.

"I was kidding," Willow said. "Bring back your super-cute excited face. Tell me more about taking over Pokémon gyms and gummy worm dioramas and video game marathons and how you did all this without kissing this boy, not even once."

I laughed. "He left when we were thirteen."

"And?"

I dug through the top drawer of my dresser and scooped up a handful of socks. I threw them in the air like confetti. "And now he's coming back!"

"For three weeks," she reminded me. "Where you will be crammed in an RV together. Sounds"—she picked up a sock ball from where it had landed on the floor next to her and half-heartedly threw it in the air—"fun?"

"This trip is going to be amazing. I get to see my child-hood best friend. I get to visit my future college. It's like my past"—I held up my left hand—"and my future"—I held up my right—"are coming together!" I joined my hands in a dramatic clap.

"What did you just do with your hands? That didn't look good. Are you getting in a major traffic accident on this trip?"

I frowned at my hands, which were still clasped, fingers intertwined. "No, it represents a magical combination where magical things are going to happen."

"It looked like a major collision—glass and twisted metal everywhere."

I rolled my eyes. "You really are jealous."

"Yes, I am. He will not take back best friend status from me. I will fight him to the death for it."

"Weapon of choice?" I asked, collecting the socks, then dropping them in my suitcase.

"Probably a long sword. Or a throwing ax. It depends. Is he tall?"

"He wasn't four years ago."

My phone buzzed on the bed with a text. Behind me, Willow's phone buzzed too. It was a message from Leena in our group text. *Who's going to the party this weekend?*

My initial instinct was to type, *Not me, I'll be in a magical collision with my childhood friend.* But that was dumb. Nobody else would get that and I'd sound ridiculous. I only said stuff like that around people I felt perfectly comfortable with, like Willow . . . and Skyler. I never worried about how I sounded around Skyler; he was just as weird as I was.

I looked out the window again, my anticipation almost unbearable now, but the street was still empty. My phone buzzed.

I'm in, Willow had answered. She wasn't one to analyze everything she said.

I'll be out of town, I finally typed. A perfectly normal response.

"You won't have to fight him," I said, back to our conversation. "Like you said, it's only three weeks. And technically we won't be crammed anywhere together. He's going to be in an RV with his mom and siblings, and I'm going to be in our RV with Mom and Ezra." But Skyler was coming to see me! Well, not specifically to see me, but it felt that way.

"Why now?" Willow asked.

"What?" I studied my suitcase and the backpack beside it, trying to decide if I had remembered everything I'd need. I had my sketch pad and pencils. Skyler would want to see all my drawings. He'd be surprised at how much better I'd gotten. I hoped he brought his sketch pad, too, so we could draw together like we used to. I'd even brought the charcoal pencil he'd loaned me before he left that I'd forgotten to give back.

Willow's voice drew my eyes out of my suitcase. "You said your moms have been talking about doing an RV trip since they were in college."

"Yeah."

"So why spring it on you now? After all these years?"

"They miss each other. Apparently, they've been planning it for months. They wanted to surprise us." I pulled my stack of flash cards from my back pocket and held them up. "Plus, I told you, I have my college interview thing."

"That's a weekend trip, not a three-week, multi-stop, bring-two-families-together-who-haven't-seen-each-other-in-years kind of thing."

"It's just another good excuse to do it now. That's all I'm saying."

"Truuue . . ." Willow crawled over to my bookshelf in the corner and started running her finger along the spines of books, pulling several out as she did and setting them aside.

"Why did you say *true* like that?"

"That's how I say *true*."

"That was a suspicious *true*." I pocketed my cards again. "Speaking of my college tour and interview, what do you think of this outfit?" I grabbed the hanger from my closet that held the pencil skirt, button-down, and blazer my mom had bought me the week before.

"Are you applying to be their librarian? Or maybe just run the school?"

"I'm serious, what do you think?"

"I think no wannabe video game animator I know would ever wear that."

"How many do you know?"

"Just you. And you don't wear that."

I laid the outfit flat across the contents of my suitcase. "You want me to wear a T-shirt and leggings to the interview?"

"Yes, your *Super Mario Bros.* Princess Peach shirt would be perfect."

I didn't even wear that to school. Besides, this was an interview. I needed to be professional, show I was serious. "Maybe Dean Collins hates *Super Mario.* Maybe she's more a *Street Fighter* fan. I can't create controversy from the very first impression."

She rolled her whole head to show she disagreed, then pointed to the stack of books she had created. "Can I borrow these while you're gone?"

"Yes."

"Cool." She stood and slid the books into her bag by the door. "And you were right about my *true.* It was suspicious."

"I know. So talk."

She looked in the mirror above my dresser and patted her dark curls. Willow was beautiful, dark brown skin, full lips, intense eyes, and curves for days. "I just think that there's probably another reason for this sudden RV trip that doesn't include husbands."

"You consider something that took at least six months to plan 'sudden'?"

"They told you two weeks ago."

"That's what a surprise is," I said. "And I've heard about this plan pretty much my whole life. It was always supposed to be husbandless. Believe me, my dad is not offended. He's been on plenty of RV trips."

"You're probably right. You know me, always suspicious. But prepare yourself for some big news in the next three weeks, just in case this trip has some hidden agenda."

"Like what?" I asked, my brain suddenly creating possibilities at her suggestion.

"As long as they don't tell you that you're moving to Ohio to join your ex–best friend, I'll be okay."

"*You'll* be okay?"

"Yes."

I picked a stuffed animal off my bed and threw it at her.

She caught it and studied the embroidered eyes of Donkey Kong. "Maybe take him to the interview?" She turned him to face me. "Is he the one that climbed a building to save that woman in distress?" She chucked him toward my bed, and he landed perfectly in my suitcase.

"You're thinking King Kong, and I'm pretty sure he *caused* her distress. But Donkey Kong is no prince either." I tossed him back in my pile. "If I were to take anyone to my interview, it would be Ms. Pac-Man. She's a baddie."

"Like you're going to be in that interview."

I took a deep breath. I hoped she was right. I would just have to focus, not go off track like my brain sometimes did, and stick to my rehearsed answers. I'd be fine.

ABOUT THE AUTHOR

KASIE WEST is the author of many YA novels, including *Places We've Never Been, Sunkissed, The Fill-in Boyfriend, P.S. I Like You, Lucky in Love,* and *Listen to Your Heart.* Her books have been named ALA Quick Picks for Reluctant Readers, Junior Library Guild selections, and YALSA Best Books for Young Adults. When she's not writing, she's binge-watching television, devouring books, or road-tripping to new places. Kasie lives in Fresno, California, with her family.

kasiewest.com

Underlined

A Community of Book Nerds & Aspiring Writers!

READ

Get book recommendations, reading lists, YA news

DISCOVER

Take quizzes, watch videos, shop merch, win prizes

CREATE

Write your own stories, enter contests, get inspired

SHARE

Connect with fellow Book Nerds and authors!

GetUnderlined.com • @GetUnderlined

Want a chance to be featured? Use #GetUnderlined on social!